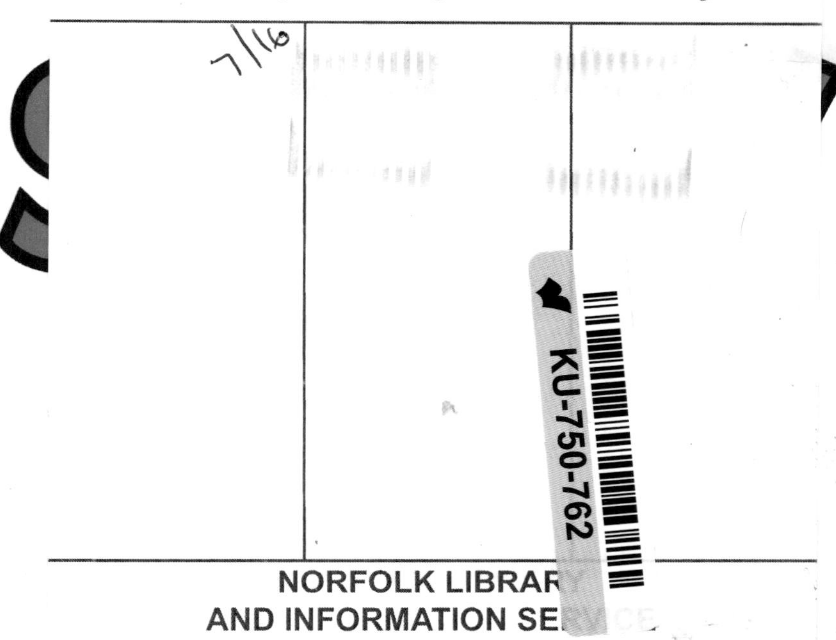

Andrews McMeel Publishing®

Kansas City • Sydney • London

CONTACT!

HOW CAN YOU BE HAPPY WHEN YOU DON'T KNOW WHAT THIS YEAR HAS IN STORE FOR YOU?

DON'T YOU WORRY ABOUT ALL THE THINGS THAT CAN HAPPEN?

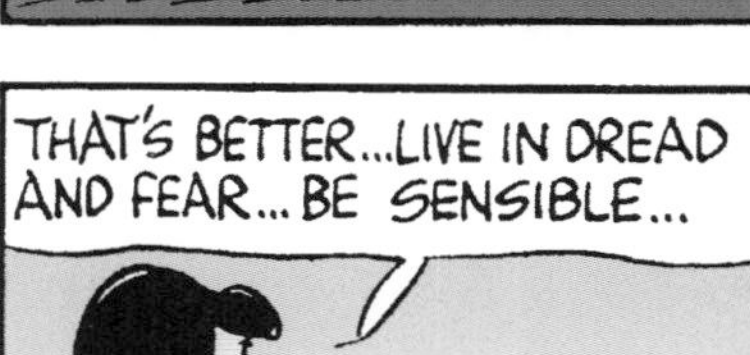
THAT'S BETTER...LIVE IN DREAD AND FEAR... BE SENSIBLE...

HE HE HE HE HE HE HE HE
SCHULZ

ALL RIGHT! CUT IT OUT!

I ALWAYS THOUGHT MAKING SNOWMEN WAS SUPPOSED TO BE FUN..
SCHULZ

SCHULZ

YOU KNOW WHAT I JUST DID? I JUST HUGGED A KITTEN!

KITTENS ARE WARM, TOO, YOU KNOW!

BLEAH!
SCHULZ

CONTACT!

HERE I AM IN MY SOPWITH CAMEL FLYING HIGH OVER FRANCE...

I SCAN THE AIR CAREFULLY SEARCHING FOR THE RED BARON.. I MUST BRING HIM DOWN!

AH, HA! THERE HE IS!

THIS TIME I'VE GOT YOU, RED BARON! THIS TIME YOU'RE MINE!

TAKE THAT! AND THAT, AND THAT, AND THAT, AND

I HATE THAT RED BARON!
SCHULZ

WELL, DON'T JUST STAND THERE...
GO GET A SHOVEL, AND HELP ME!

SCHULZ

AAUGH!

WHEW

I THINK MY FEET
NEED SHARPENING...
SCHULZ

!
?
I THOUGHT I HEARD SOMETHING

GOOD GRIEF! SOMEONE'S PROWLING AROUND IN MY HOUSE!

WHAT IF IT'S A..A..A...

CAT BURGLAR?!
SCHULZ

THERE'S A BURGLAR IN MY HOUSE!

OH, WHY DO I LIVE ALONE? I COULD HAVE BEEN MURDERED IN MY BED! THIS IS AWFUL!

HOW DID HE GET IN? WHY DIDN'T ANYONE SOUND THE ALARM? WHAT'S WRONG WITH THE STUPID WATCHDOG?

I'M THE STUPID WATCHDOG!
SCHULZ

THERE'S A BURGLAR DOWN THERE...I CAN HEAR HIM!

I CAN HEAR **TWO** OF THEM! I WONDER WHAT THEY'RE AFTER.. MAYBE MY SILVER CANDLESTICKS...

THEY'RE COMING UP THE STAIRWAY!

THEY'RE STEALING MY VAN GOGH!
SCHULZ

ART THIEVES!

CAN YOU IMAGINE THOSE TWO BIRDS? THEY THOUGHT THEY COULD SNEAK INTO MY HOME, AND STEAL MY VALUABLE VAN GOGH!

WELL, I SURE SHOWED THEM! A LITTLE MANUAL LABOR WILL TEACH THEM A LESSON...

DIG, THIEVES, DIG!
SCHULZ

HERE'S THE WORLD WAR I PILOT FLYING HIS "SOPWITH CAMEL"...

TODAY I'M FLYING OVER BELGIUM...I CAN SEE AN ARMY CONVOY BELOW...

BUT I MUST SEARCH OUT THE INFAMOUS RED BARON, AND BRING HIM DOWN !

AAUGH! THERE HE IS ON MY TAIL! HE'S TRICKED ME AGAIN!

MY PLANE IS ON FIRE!!

I'VE GOT TO BAIL OUT!

CURSE YOU, RED BARON!

WHEN BAILING OUT, THE AVERAGE WORLD WAR I FIGHTER PILOT DID NOT LAND IN HIS SUPPER DISH!
HOW EMBARRASSING!
SCHULZ

RATS!

THEY NEVER HAVE ANY PROGRAMS THAT I LIKE..

I WONDER WHY NO ONE PUTS OUT WHAT I WOULD CONSIDER A PERFECT PROGRAM...

A FOUR-HOUR DOCUMENTARY ON BEAGLES!
SCHULZ

HERE'S THE WORLD WAR I FLYING ACE POSING BESIDE HIS SOPWITH CAMEL

I AM TAKING OFF FROM AN AERODROME IN FRANCE SOMEWHERE JUST EAST OF PONT-À-MOUSSON...

MY MISSION IS TO SEEK OUT THE RED BARON, AND TO BRING HIM DOWN! **CONTACT!**

SO LONG, CHAPS! WISH ME LUCK!
MY DOG HAS FINALLY FLIPPED!
SCHULZ

HERE'S THE WORLD WAR I FLYING ACE ZOOMING THROUGH THE AIR SEARCHING FOR THE 'RED BARON'

AS I PASS OVER METZ, ENEMY BATTERIES BEGIN FIRING...SHELLS BURST BELOW MY SOPWITH CAMEL..

NYAHH, NYAHH, NYAHH!! YOU CAN'T HIT ME!

ACTUALLY, TOUGH FLYING ACES NEVER SAY, 'NYAHH, NYAHH, NYAHH!'
SCHULZ

HERE I AM FLYING HIGH OVER ENEMY LINES IN MY SOPWITH CAMEL SEARCHING FOR THE "RED BARON"

WHO'S THAT BEHIND ME?

IT'S THE RED BARON! HE HAS ME IN HIS SIGHTS!!

GIVE MY REGARDS TO BROADWAY
SCHULZ

HERE'S THE WORLD WAR I PILOT TAKING OFF FROM A FIELD SOMEWHERE IN ENGLAND...

DRAT THIS FOG! IT'S BAD ENOUGH HAVING TO FIGHT THE RED BARON WITHOUT FIGHTING THE FOG, TOO!

HEADQUARTERS EXPECTS TOO MUCH OF US...WHEN I GET BACK, I THINK I'LL WRITE A LETTER TO PRESIDENT WILSON

IT'S THE "RED BARON"! HE'S GOT ME AGAIN!

CURSE YOU, RED BARON!

I'VE GOT TO MAKE A FORCED LANDING BEHIND THE TRENCHES...

BRUISED AND BATTERED I CRAWL OUT OF MY WRECKED SOPWITH CAMEL... I'M TRAPPED IN THE MIDDLE OF NO-MAN'S LAND! SLOWLY I CREEP FORWARD...

SUDDENLY, THERE IT IS.... BARBED WIRE!!! I'VE GOT TO GET THROUGH IT BEFORE THE MACHINE GUNNERS SEE ME..

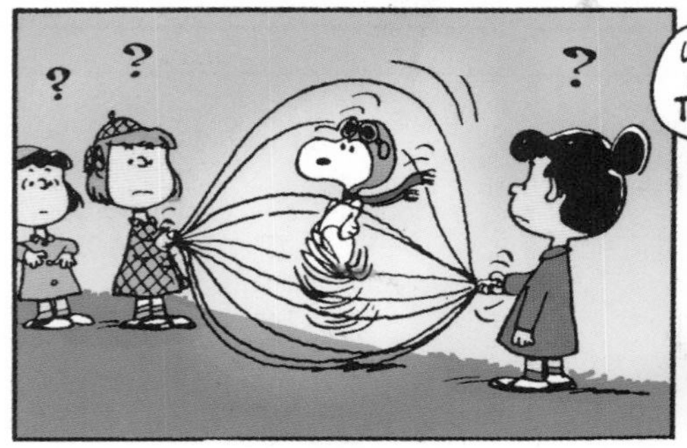
?
?
?

WHAT WAS THAT?
I THINK IT WAS A WORLD WAR I PILOT GOING THROUGH SOME BARBED WIRE, BUT I'M NOT SURE...
SCHULZ

THE RED BARON HAS HIT MY PLANE!

I'M FORCED TO MAKE A HAVE LANDING...I MEAN I'M LANDING TO A HAVE FORCED...

I MEAN I'M HAVING TO FORCE A ...I'M MAKING A HAVE... A FORCED I'M ...I'M...

CURSE YOU, RED BARON!
SCHULZ

HERE'S THE WORLD WAR I PILOT DOWN BEHIND ENEMY LINES..

SUDDENLY I SEE AN ENEMY SOLDIER! IT LOOKS LIKE A SENTRY...IF I CAN GET PAST HIM, I CAN MAKE IT BACK TO MY SQUADRON...I'LL SNEAK UP ON HIM, AND FLIP HIM OVER MY SHOULDER.. EASY NOW...EASY....

AAUGH!

SCHULZ

HERE'S THE PILOT LYING IN HIS BUNK MAKING A SOLEMN AND DETERMINED VOW...

HERE'S "BEAU" SNOOPY OF THE FOREIGN LEGION MARCHING ACROSS THE DESERT

NOTHING BUT SAND AS FAR AS THE EYE CAN SEE...BUZZARDS CIRCLE OVERHEAD...WATER! WE MUST HAVE WATER! WATER...

HERE...YOU LOOKED KIND OF THIRSTY SO I BROUGHT YOU YOUR DISH

WHAT FUN IS THAT?
SCHULZ

WHO ELSE DO YOU KNOW WHO CAN DO THE "BEAGLE"?
SCHULZ

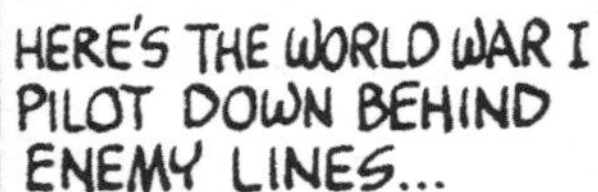
HERE'S THE WORLD WAR I PILOT DOWN BEHIND ENEMY LINES...

BY NIGHT I SNEAK THROUGH THE ABANDONED TRENCHES..

BY DAY I SLEEP ON HAYSTACKS...

SUDDENLY IT'S NIGHT AGAIN...I MUST CONTINUE MY JOURNEY ACROSS FRANCE TO REACH THE CHANNEL...

WHAT'S THIS? A SMALL FRENCH FARM HOUSE! ANYBODY HOME?

AH, MADEMOISELLE...DO NOT BE AFRAID..I AM A PILOT WITH THE ALLIES.. MY PLANE WAS SHOT DOWN BY THE RED BARON...

SHE DOES NOT UNDERSTAND ZE ENGLISH...AH, BUT SHE WILL UNDERSTAND THAT I AM A HANDSOME YOUNG PILOT...

AND SHE? SHE IS A BEAUTIFUL FRENCH GIRL.. SOUP? AH, YES, MADEMOISELLE, THAT WOULD BE WONDERFUL! A LITTLE POTATO SOUP, AND I WILL BE ON MY WAY...

BUT HOW CAN I BEAR TO LEAVE HER? PERHAPS SOMEDAY I CAN RETURN..AU REVOIR, MADEMOISELLE..AU REVOIR! AH, WHAT A PITY...HER HEART IS BREAKING... DO NOT CRY, LITTLE ONE.. DO NOT CRY...

FAREWELL! FAREWELL!

CURSE THE RED BARON AND HIS KIND! CURSE THE WICKEDNESS IN THIS WORLD! CURSE THE EVIL THAT CAUSES ALL THIS UNHAPPINESS! CURSE THE..

I THINK THESE MISSIONS ARE GETTING TO BE TOO MUCH FOR HIM..
SCHULZ

I HATE TO THINK ABOUT IT... THE RESPONSIBILITY SCARES ME TO DEATH.. I WISH YOU HADN'T BROUGHT IT UP...

I DON'T THINK HE KNOWS THAT MY SOPWITH CAMEL IS POWERED BY A ROTARY ENGINE WITH A RIGHT-HAND TORQUE SO I CAN EVADE HIM BY TURNING HARD TO THE RIGHT **WITH** THE PULL OF MY ENGINE....

HERE I AM IN MY SOPWITH CAMEL FLYING 15,000 FEET OVER ENEMY LINES...

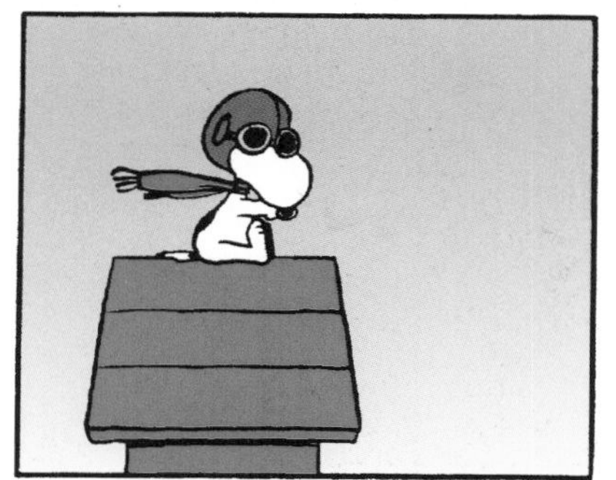

15,000 FEET?

I FEEL SICK...
SCHULZ

IT'S BEEN A LONG TIME SINCE I'VE BITTEN SOMEONE ON THE LEG...

CLOMP!

MY TIMING IS WAY OFF...
SCHULZ

HERE'S THE WORLD WAR I FLYING ACE TAKING OFF IN HIS SOPWITH CAMEL..

I AM HEADING FOR THE ENEMY LINES ALONE DETERMINED TO FIND THE RED BARON!

I FLY OVER VERDUN AND FORT DOUAUMONT...THEN I TURN EAST TOWARD ETAIN...THE SUN IS DIRECTLY IN MY EYES...

GREAT SCOTT! IT'S THE RED BARON AND THE ENTIRE FLYING CIRCUS!!

I CAN'T STAND THEM ALONE! I'VE GOT TO RUN! GO, CAMEL, GO!!!

THEY'RE RIGHT BEHIND ME! THEY'RE ALL AROUND ME! I'M SURROUNDED BY FOKKER TRIPLANES!

AUGH!

WHY CAN'T I HAVE A DOG WHO DOES SIMPLE THINGS LIKE CHASING CARS?
SCHULZ

YOU'RE SITTING HERE WAITING TO CHOMP SOMEONE ON THE LEG, AREN'T YOU?

ALL RIGHT, GO AHEAD, AND CHOMP, BUT WHEN YOU DO, YOU'RE GOING TO BE SORRY!

TO CHOMP OR NOT TO CHOMP.. THAT IS THE QUESTION!
SCHULZ

I DON'T SUPPOSE YOU'D BE INTERESTED IN CHASING A FEW RABBITS TODAY, WOULD YOU?

SOME QUESTIONS AREN'T EVEN WORTH ANSWERING
SCHULZ

Z

?
Z

I DON'T SEE HOW HE CAN SLEEP LIKE THAT..
Z

MY HEAD'S ASLEEP, BUT MY FEET ARE AWAKE!
Z
SCHULZ

HERE'S THE WORLD WAR I PILOT ASLEEP IN HIS BUNK..

SUDDENLY HE IS AWAKENED! IT'S TIME TO FLY ANOTHER DAWN PATROL..

AT THREE O'CLOCK IN THE MORNING?!!

TELL PRESIDENT WILSON TO CALL ME AT TEN!
SCHULZ

RATS!

HE ALWAYS PUTS TOO MUCH CINNAMON ON MY CINNAMON TOAST!
SCHULZ

EVERY NIGHT IT'S THE SAME..

I HAVE SUPPER IN MY RED DISH AND DRINKING WATER IN MY YELLOW DISH...

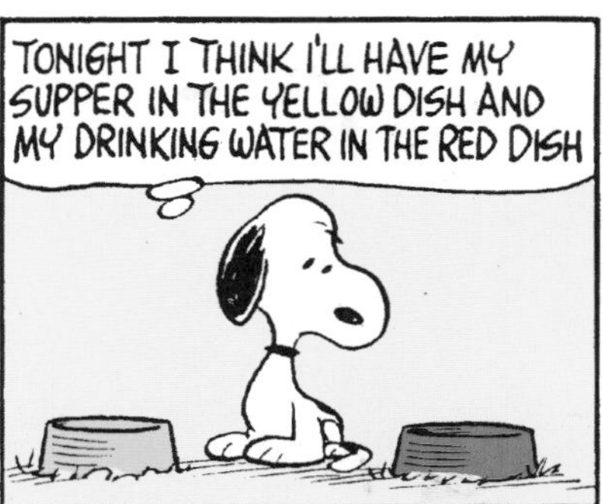
TONIGHT I THINK I'LL HAVE MY SUPPER IN THE YELLOW DISH AND MY DRINKING WATER IN THE RED DISH

LIFE IS TOO SHORT NOT TO LIVE IT UP A LITTLE!
SCHULZ

I ALWAYS ENJOY SPECULATING ON WHAT OUR LIFE WOULD BE LIKE IF YOU AND I EVER GOT MARRIED, SCHROEDER...

I'LL BET WE'D HAVE A SON..AND HE'D PROBABLY BE A GREAT MUSICIAN JUST LIKE YOU...

BUT I WONDER WHAT HE'D LOOK LIKE... I WONDER IF HE'D HAVE MY SENSITIVE EXPRESSION...

WHAT DO YOU THINK OUR SON WOULD LOOK LIKE?

WELL, PERHAPS.....BUT I'D LIKE TO THINK THAT HIS NOSE WOULDN'T BE QUITE THAT BIG...
SCHULZ

I'LL THROW THE STICK, AND YOU CHASE IT, OKAY?

I THOUGHT I'D BETTER LEAVE BEFORE I LOST MY COOL...
SCHULZ

OVER THERE! OVER THERE!

PACK UP YOUR TROUBLES IN YOUR OLD KIT BAG...

IT'S A LONG WAY TO TIPPERARY....

WE WORLD WAR I FLYING ACES ARE VERY SENTIMENTAL...
SCHULZ

ARE YOU GOING TO HANG ONTO THAT BLANKET FOR THE REST OF YOUR LIFE?

DON'T BE RIDICULOUS..SOMEDAY I'LL JUST TOSS IT AWAY LIKE THAT...

SOMEDAY!

I REFUSE TO CHASE A STICK THAT HASN'T BEEN PROPERLY SANDED AND POLISHED!

!

SUPPERTIME!

SUPPERTIME!

OH, IT'S SUPPERTIME! IT'S SUPPERTIME!!!

YAHOO! IT'S SUPPERTIME!

SUPPERTIME! SUPPERTIME! SUPPERTIME!
GOOD OL' SUP, SUP, SUP, SUPPERTIME!

SUPPERTIME!

I MUST ADMIT HE'S A VERY SATISFYING PERSON TO COOK FOR
SCHULZ

WHERE'S MY BEACH BALL?

I CAME TO THE LAKE TO ENJOY MYSELF, AND RIGHT AWAY MY BEACH BALL DISAPPEARS!

ALL RIGHT, WHO'S GOT MY BEACH BALL?

SCHULZ

LICK
LICK
LICK
LICK
LICK

LAP
LAP
LAP
LAP
LAP
LAP

LICK
LAP
LICK
LAP
LICK
LAP

I KNEW I HEARD AN ICE CREAM CONE APPROACHING
LICK
LICK
LICK
LICK
LICK
SCHULZ

WHAT ARE "DOG DAYS"?

"DOG DAYS" ARE CALCULATED BY THE RISING OF SIRIUS, THE DOG-STAR. THEY BEGIN AROUND JULY 3RD AND END SOMEWHERE AROUND AUGUST 11TH

PEOPLE USED TO BELIEVE THAT "DOG DAYS" WERE SO NAMED BECAUSE DOGS GOT RABIES DURING THE HOT WEATHER, BUT THIS, OF COURSE, ISN'T TRUE

I'M OFF THE HOOK
SCHULZ

HERE'S THE WORLD WAR I FLYING ACE WALKING ONTO THE FIELD.."GOOD MORNING, CHAPS!" (THESE ARE GOOD LADS)

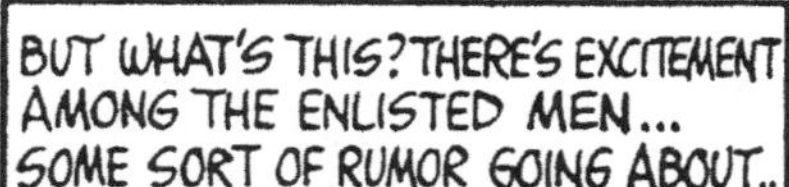
BUT WHAT'S THIS? THERE'S EXCITEMENT AMONG THE ENLISTED MEN... SOME SORT OF RUMOR GOING ABOUT..

HERE'S THE FLYING ACE REPORTING TO HIS COMMANDING OFFICER... "GOOD MORNING, SIR..A ROOT BEER? YES, SIR, I DON'T MIND IF I DO"

THERE MUST BE SOMETHING BIG COMING UP... HE ONLY OFFERS ME A ROOT BEER WHEN THERE'S A DANGEROUS MISSION TO BE FLOWN!
SCHULZ

THIS IS GREAT FOR HIM..HE'LL SIT HERE ALL DAY AS LONG AS I SCRATCH HIS HEAD...
SCRATCH SCRATCH SCRATCH

BUT WHAT DO I GET OUT OF IT? A HANDFUL OF TIRED FINGERS, THAT'S WHAT I GET OUT OF IT!
SKRITCH SKRITCH SKRITCH SKRITCH

I STAND HERE SCRATCHING AND SCRATCHING AND SCRATCHING..I DO ALL THE WORK WHILE HE JUST SITS THERE..SOMETIMES I THINK HE TAKES ADVANTAGE OF ME
SKRATCH SKRATCH SKRATCH

I'LL END UP GETTING TENDINITIS OR SOMETHING, AND HAVE TO GO TO A DOCTOR AND GET A SHOT... I COULD STAND HERE UNTIL BOTH MY ARMS FALL OFF FOR ALL HE CARES... GOOD GRIEF!
SKRITCH SKRITCH SKRITCH SKRITCH

I'M THE SORT OF PERSON PEOPLE JUST NATURALLY TAKE ADVANTAGE OF... THAT'S THE TROUBLE WITH THIS WORLD... HALF THE PEOPLE ARE THE KIND WHO TAKE ADVANTAGE OF THE OTHER HALF!
SKRITCHY SKRITCHY SKRITCHY

WELL, I'M NOT GOING TO BE THE KIND WHO GETS TAKEN ADVANTAGE OF! I'M NOT GOING TO JUST STAND HERE AND SCRATCH HIS HEAD FOREVER
SKROETCH SKROETCH SKROETCH

I REFUSE TO LET SOMEONE TAKE ADVANTAGE OF ME THIS WAY...I'M NOT GOING TO LET HIM DO IT... I MEAN, WHY SHOULD I?
SCROOTCH SCROOTCH SCROOTCH

I'M JUST THE SORT OF PERSON PEOPLE NATURALLY TAKE ADVANTAGE OF....
SKRITCH SKRITCH SKRITCH SKRITCH
SCHULZ

HERE'S THE WORLD WAR I FLYING ACE TALKING WITH HIS COMMANDING OFFICER...

"ON OUR LEFT IS ST. MIHIEL... ON OUR RIGHT IS PONT-A-MOUSSON... INTELLIGENCE REPORTS THAT AN AMMUNITION TRAIN IS AT THE RAILWAY STATION IN LONGUYON..."

"OUR BOMBERS CANNOT GET THROUGH, BUT ONE LONE AIRPLANE FLYING VERY LOW JUST MIGHT MAKE IT..."

I, OF COURSE, VOLUNTEER!
SCHULZ

IT'S DAWN... A FINE MIST COVERS THE FRENCH COUNTRYSIDE..

THE WORLD WAR I FLYING ACE CLIMBS INTO HIS SOPWITH CAMEL.. THIS IS HIS MOST DANGEROUS MISSION! AN AMMUNITION TRAIN MUST BE DESTROYED AND ONE LONE PLANE MUST DO THE JOB!

"SWITCH OFF" YELLS THE MECHANIC... "COUPEZ" I REPLY.. "CONTACT?" "CONTACT IT IS!" THE MOTOR CATCHES WITH A ROAR!
RRRRRR

MOMENTS LATER I AM FLYING LOW OVER THE MOSELLE
RRRRRRR
FOUR O'CLOCK IN THE MORNING.. HOW DO YOU EXPLAIN THIS TO THE NEIGHBORS?
SCHULZ

HERE'S THE WORLD WAR I PILOT FLYING LOW OVER ENEMY LINES..

STARTLED ENEMY SOLDIERS LOOK UP AS I ZOOM OVERHEAD, BUT BY THE TIME THEY SEE ME...

BLEAH!!
BLEAH! BLEAH! BLEAH!

...IT IS TOO LATE!
SCHULZ

HERE'S THE WORLD WAR I PILOT FLYING LOW OVER ENEMY TERRITORY...

MY MISSION IS TO FIND THE AMMUNITION TRAIN IN LONGUYON, AND DESTROY IT...

SUDDENLY GROUND FIRE BURSTS ALL AROUND ME! MY SOPWITH CAMEL IS HIT!

"IT'S A LONG WAY TO TIPPERARY"
SCHULZ

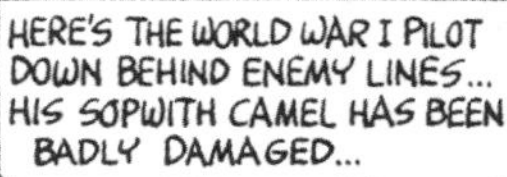

HERE'S THE WORLD WAR I PILOT DOWN BEHIND ENEMY LINES... HIS SOPWITH CAMEL HAS BEEN BADLY DAMAGED...

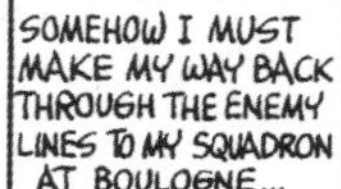

SOMEHOW I MUST MAKE MY WAY BACK THROUGH THE ENEMY LINES TO MY SQUADRON AT BOULOGNE...

OH, GOOD GRIEF, IT'S TIME TO FEED THE DOG AGAIN..

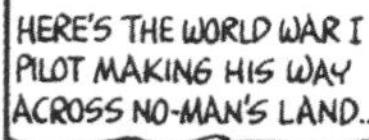

HERE'S THE WORLD WAR I PILOT MAKING HIS WAY ACROSS NO-MAN'S LAND..

WHAT'S THAT UP AHEAD? OH, NO! AN ENEMY TANK! I MUST DESTROY IT!

A GRENADE OUGHT TO DO IT! ONE GRENADE RIGHT ON THE OL' TARGET!! I PULL THE PIN..

I HURL THE GRENADE
BWANG!
SPLUT!

I HATE WORLD WAR I! I HATE THE RED BARON! I HATE SOPWITH CAMELS! I HATE FLYING BEAGLES! I HATE....
SCHULZ

HERE'S THE WORLD WAR I PILOT DOWN BEHIND ENEMY LINES...

WHAT'S THE CHAIN FOR, CHARLIE BROWN?
I HAVE TO CATCH SNOOPY, AND TAKE HIM TO THE VET'S FOR A SHOT...

SLOWLY I SNEAK FORWARD..ENEMY SOLDIERS ARE ALL AROUND ME...BUT THEY'LL NEVER TAKE ME ALIVE...I SHALL NEVER SURRENDER...I SHALL..

COMRADE!!
SCHULZ

WHAT ARE YOU DOING?
I HAVE TO TAKE SNOOPY TO THE VET'S FOR A SHOT..
RATS! CAPTURED BY THE ENEMY!

THEY WON'T GET ANY INFORMATION FROM ME!

I'LL JUST PRETEND TO COOPERATE...

I WISH HE WOULDN'T DO THAT.. IT'S VERY EMBARRASSING...
SCHULZ

A DESPERATE BID FOR FREEDOM!
OOF!!

AS THE ESCAPING PILOT FLEES ACROSS THE COUNTRYSIDE, HE SUDDENLY SPOTS THE AMMUNITION TRAIN HE WAS SENT TO DESTROY!

HE LEAPS ON THE ENGINEER! THE TRAIN IS DERAILED!

HERE'S THE WORLD WAR I PILOT RACING ACROSS NO MAN'S LAND TO REJOIN HIS OUTFIT! SHELLS BURST! BULLETS FLY!
CHARLIE BROWN, WHY DON'T YOU TRY RAISING GOLDFISH OR SOMETHING?
SCHULZ

DID YOU CATCH SNOOPY AGAIN, CHARLIE BROWN?

YEAH, WE FINALLY CAUGHT HIM... WE DRAGGED HIM OVER TO THE VET, AND HE GOT HIS SHOT..

WHAT A STRUGGLE!

THEY TORTURED ME, BUT ALL I GAVE THEM WAS MY NAME, RANK AND SERIAL NUMBER!
SCHULZ

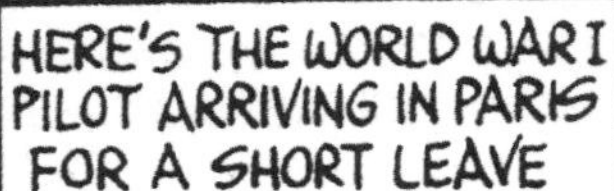
HERE'S THE WORLD WAR I PILOT ARRIVING IN PARIS FOR A SHORT LEAVE

AH, PARIS! WHAT A GLORIOUS SIGHT!

WHAT'S THIS? A SMALL SIDEWALK CAFE...

HOW GOOD IT IS TO BE AWAY FROM THE SOUNDS OF BATTLE... TO SIT HERE IN THE SUN...

GARÇON! A ROOT BEER, PLEASE!

PERHAPS MADEMOISELLE WOULD CARE TO JOIN ME IN A ROOT BEER?

SHE IS DAZZLED BY THE HANDSOME PILOT OF THE ALLIES... AH, THE WAR SEEMS SO FAR AWAY....

BUT THIS IS OUTRAGEOUS! I CAN'T SIT HERE WITH THIS BEAUTIFUL FRENCH GIRL WHILE MY BUDDIES ARE FIGHTING THE RED BARON!

AH, MY LITTLE ONE, YOU ARE GOING TO MISS ME, NO? BUT I MUST GO...DO NOT WEEP..... PLEASE, DO NOT HANG ONTO MY TUNIC...

THIS IS WHERE I BELONG! HIGH ABOVE THE CLOUDS SEARCHING FOR THE RED BARON!

!

I SHOULD HAVE STAYED IN PARIS...
SCHULZ

I CAN'T SIT LIKE THIS FOREVER.. MY NECK IS GETTING STIFF!
Z

ON THE OTHER HAND, IF I MOVE, HE'LL BUMP HIS HEAD... IT'S EITHER MY NECK OR HIS HEAD...
Z

KLUNK!

IT WAS AN EASY CHOICE TO MAKE!
SCHULZ

SNIF?
I SMELL SMOKE!
SNIF SNIF

BAM! BAM! BAM! BAM!

WHAT IN THE WORLD.....

GOOD GRIEF!
MY BOOKS! MY RECORDS! MY POOL TABLE! MY VAN GOGH!
SOB!
SCHULZ

WAAH!
SCHULZ

SCHULZ

ACCORDING TO THIS, YOUR FIRE INSURANCE HAS LAPSED!

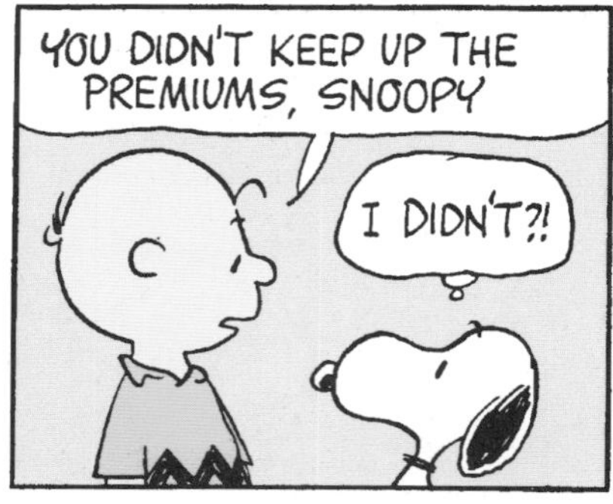
YOU DIDN'T KEEP UP THE PREMIUMS, SNOOPY
I DIDN'T?!

HOW COULD THAT BE?

I SENT THEM A CAN OF DOG FOOD EVERY MONTH!
SCHULZ

THIS IS RIDICULOUS!
SCHULZ

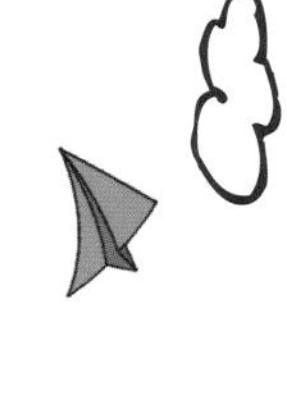

WELL, HERE'S THE LIST OF ALL THE THINGS YOU LOST IN THE FIRE

ALL THE CARPETING WAS RUINED, OF COURSE, AND THE POOL TABLE IS SHOT...YOUR WHOLE LIBRARY IS GONE, AND YOUR VAN GOGH IS DESTROYED...

ACTUALLY, SNOOPY, EVERYTHING IS GONE!

EVEN MY PINKING SHEARS?!
SCHULZ

HERE'S THE WORLD WAR I FLYING ACE REPORTING FOR DUTY

HIS MISSION TODAY IS TO SEARCH OUT THE RED BARON, AND BRING HIM DOWN..HE CROSSES THE FIELD TO HIS SOPWITH CAMEL..

WHAT SOPWITH CAMEL?!
SCHULZ

THESE ARE THE PLANS FOR SNOOPY'S NEW HOME...

IT'S A BIT MUCH, ISN'T IT? AFTER ALL, HE'S ONLY A STUPID DOG!

BOOT!

NOW, HERE IS WHERE WE'LL BE USING THE CERAMIC TILE, AND THIS STAIRWAY IS THE ONE I WAS TELLING YOU ABOUT..
I LOVE LOOKING AT HOUSE PLANS!
SCHULZ

THERE YOU ARE, SNOOPY...YOUR NEW HOUSE IS ALL FINISHED..

WELL, WHAT DO YOU THINK?

IT'S BEAUTIFUL!
SNIF!
SCHULZ

I CAN'T SLEEP...

I GUESS I'M JUST KIND OF NERVOUS...

IT'S ALWAYS EXCITING WHEN YOU SPEND YOUR FIRST NIGHT ON A NEW HOME!
SCHULZ

HERE'S THE WORLD WAR I FLYING ACE ZOOMING THROUGH THE AIR IN HIS SOPWITH CAMEL!

DOWN BELOW I CAN SEE THE INFANTRYMEN HUDDLED IN THEIR MUDDY TRENCHES...

POOR BLIGHTERS!

WE FLYING ACES ALWAYS CALL THEM "POOR BLIGHTERS"
SCHULZ

HERE'S THE WORLD WAR I PILOT FLYING IN HIS SOPWITH CAMEL SEARCHING FOR THE RED BARON!

DOWN BELOW I SEE THE LITTLE VILLAGE OF TOUQUIN AND THE RIVER MARNE..

THERE'S THE RED BARON! HE'S DIVING RIGHT AT ME! I'VE GOT TO..

RATS!

HERE I AM BRINGING MY WOUNDED MACHINE DOWN OVER THE FRONT LINES! WHAT COURAGE! WHAT FORTITUDE!

CRASH! MY PLANE FLIPS OVER INTO A SHELL HOLE!

I MUST REPORT BACK TO MY SQUADRON COMMANDER...HE'LL BE GLAD TO SEE ME...
KNOCK KNOCK

FLYING ACE SNOOPY REPORTING, SIR... I..

YES, SIR..YES, SIR... I KNOW THAT, SIR..YES, SIR...YOU'RE RIGHT, SIR.. YES, SIR..YES, SIR... VERY WELL, SIR...

I'M THE ONLY PILOT WHO EVER GOT PUT ON K.P. FOR LOSING TOO MANY SOPWITH CAMELS!
SCHULZ

ARE YOU SURE YOU CAN FIND YOUR WAY HOME NOW?
ABSOLUTELY! WE WON'T HAVE ANY TROUBLE AT ALL
HERE'S THE WORLD WAR I FLYING ACE RECEIVING HIS ORDERS...

SNOOPY HAS A GOOD SENSE OF DIRECTION, DON'T YOU, SNOOPY?
THE RED BARON HAS BEEN SIGHTED OVER CAMBRAI..I MUST BRING HIM DOWN!

I SAID, YOU CAN GET US HOME, CAN'T YOU, SNOOPY?
MY FAITHFUL MECHANICS ARE STANDING BY MY SOPWITH CAMEL...THEY ADMIRE MY CONFIDENT ATTITUDE...

IF YOU DON'T HEAR FROM US, SEND OUT A ST. BERNARD!
AS I WALK ACROSS THE FIELD TO MY PLANE, EVERYONE WAVES....I WAVE BACK.."SO LONG, CHAPS! SO LONG!"
SCHULZ

THERE'S NOT ENOUGH ROOM UNDER HERE FOR ALL THREE OF US!

I KNEW THEY'D FEEL GUILTY!
SCHULZ

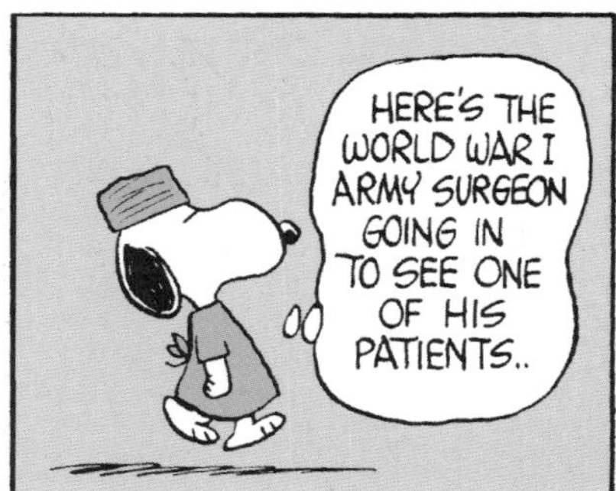

MY GROUND CREW IS PROUD OF ME... THEY LIKE TO SEND PICTURES OF ME TO THEIR GIRLS BACK HOME....

I HATE THESE PRACTICE SESSIONS!
SCHULZ

Z

GOOD GRIEF, I'M DROWNING!

Z
SCHULZ

OUR FAMILY ATE DINNER AT A RESTAURANT TONIGHT, SNOOPY

I BROUGHT YOU A SUGAR LUMP

THAT SHOULD MAKE ME HAPPY, BUT IT DOESN'T...
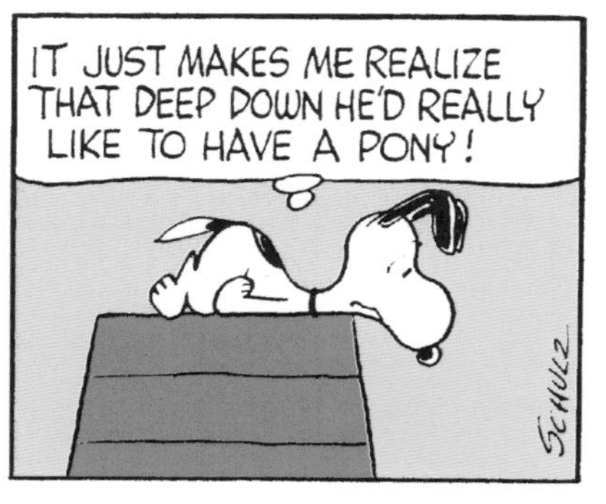
IT JUST MAKES ME REALIZE THAT DEEP DOWN HE'D REALLY LIKE TO HAVE A PONY!
SCHULZ

?
Z

OH! PARDON ME!

RIGHT IN THE MIDDLE OF A GOOD DREAM!
SCHULZ

I FEEL GUILTY ABOUT THE WAY I FEED SNOOPY...HIS MEALS ARE SO DRAB...

I SHOULD DO SOMETHING TO MAKE HIS MEALS MORE INTERESTING..
Dog Food

SCHULZ

ONE, PLEASE

ONE, PLEASE

ONE, PLEASE

ONE, PLEASE

?

I DON'T EVEN KNOW WHAT'S GOING ON!
SCHULZ

WELL, SNOOPY, WHAT ARE YOUR PLANS FOR TODAY?

PLANS? I HADN'T EVEN THOUGHT ABOUT IT...

BUT I SUPPOSE I'LL SLEEP A LITTLE THIS MORNING...THEN, THIS AFTERNOON, I'LL TAKE A SHORT NAP, AND LATER ON I'LL TRY TO GET SOME MORE SLEEP...

THOSE ARE GOOD PLANS
SCHULZ

I WORRY ABOUT THIS TIME OF YEAR..

I REMEMBER LAST YEAR ABOUT THIS TIME...IT WAS TWO O'CLOCK IN THE MORNING, AND I WAS SOUND ASLEEP...

SUDDENLY, OUT OF NOWHERE, THIS CRAZY GUY WITH A SLED LANDS RIGHT ON MY ROOF

HE WAS OKAY, BUT THOSE STUPID REINDEER KEPT STEPPING ON MY STOMACH!
SCHULZ

HERE'S THE WORLD WAR I FLYING ACE STANDING BESIDE HIS SOPWITH CAMEL

IT IS EVENING... CHOW IS OVER... HE IS ENTERTAINING THE ENLISTED MEN WITH TALES OF BRAVE DUELS FOUGHT IN THE SKY...

POOR BLIGHTERS...THEY NEED INSPIRATION AND CHEERING UP...

BUT WHO CHEERS UP THE WORLD WAR I FLYING ACE?
SCHULZ

HERE'S THE WORLD WAR I PILOT WALKING OUT ONTO THE FIELD...

SMAK

I LOVE MY SOPWITH CAMEL!
SCHULZ

I CAN'T SLEEP!

MAYBE IF I MOVE AROUND AND TRY DIFFERENT POSITIONS...

RATS! I JUST CAN'T GET COMFORTABLE!

SNOOPY?

SNOOPY?

WHERE'D HE GO?

Z
SCHULZ

GOOD GRIEF!

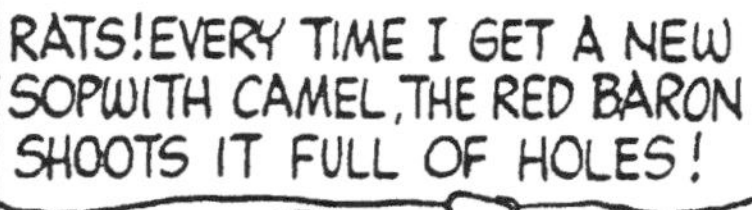
RATS! EVERY TIME I GET A NEW SOPWITH CAMEL, THE RED BARON SHOOTS IT FULL OF HOLES!

OUR SUPPLY SERGEANT HATES ME!
SCHULZ

HERE'S THE WORLD WAR I PILOT FLYING OVER ENEMY LINES...

IF I LOSE ANOTHER SOPWITH CAMEL, OUR SUPPLY SERGEANT WILL KILL ME...

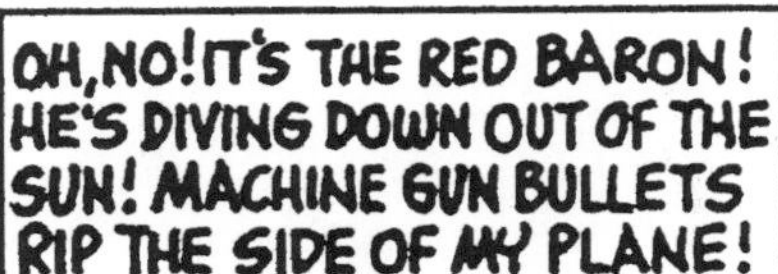
OH, NO! IT'S THE RED BARON! HE'S DIVING DOWN OUT OF THE SUN! MACHINE GUN BULLETS RIP THE SIDE OF MY PLANE!

THIS COULD RUIN MY WHOLE DAY..
SCHULZ

THEY'RE RIGHT...
IT **IS** A LONG WAY
TO TIPPERARY!
SCHULZ

HERE'S THE WORLD WAR I PILOT DOWN BEHIND ENEMY LINES...

IF I'M CAPTURED, I'LL BE SHOT AT DAWN...

I'LL SNEAK BACK INTO MY DAMAGED SOPWITH CAMEL, AND PUT ON MY SPECIAL DISGUISE..

WO IST DER ROOT BEER HALL?
SCHULZ

HERE'S THE WORLD WAR I PILOT SITTING IN A LITTLE RESTAURANT BEHIND ENEMY LINES
NO ONE RECOGNIZES ME IN MY VERY CLEVER DISGUISE

WHO'S THAT AT THE NEXT TABLE? HE LOOKS FAMILIAR.... GOOD GRIEF, IT'S THE RED BARON!

HI, RED!
SCHULZ

AH, RED BARON, AT LAST WE MEET FACE TO FACE!

THERE IS RESPECT IN YOUR EYES, NO? YES, I AM THE FAMOUS PILOT WITH THE ALLIES

PERHAPS THERE IS ALSO A LITTLE FEAR IN YOUR EYES, NO?

NO!
SCHULZ

PRISON! THEY THREW ME IN PRISON!

WHY DID I HAVE TO GIVE MYSELF AWAY IN THAT RESTAURANT? WHY DID I GO OVER AND TALK TO THE RED BARON?

NOW, I'LL SPEND THE REST OF WORLD WAR I IN THIS PRISON... THEY'LL NEVER LET ME OUT! NEVER!

OWOOOOOOO
SCHULZ

HERE'S THE WORLD WAR I PILOT LYING IN A BED AT THE BASE HOSPITAL..
Z

THE MEMORY OF THE TERRIBLE DAYS IN THE SKY DRIVES SLEEP FROM HIS MIND...HIS NERVES ARE RAW...THE SOUND OF EXPLODING ANTI-AIRCRAFT FIRE DRUMS THROUGH HIS HEAD....

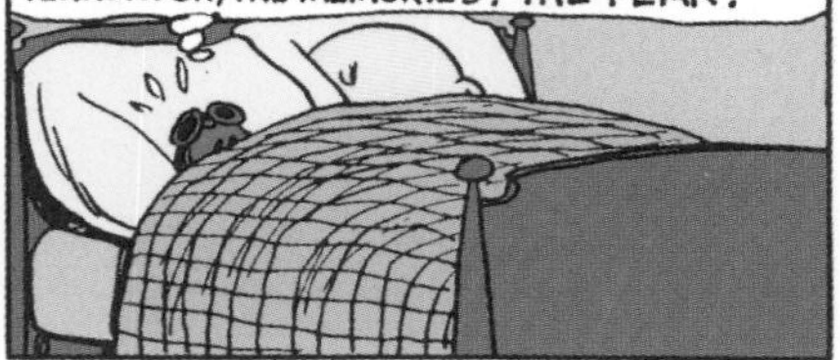
A FOKKER TRI-PLANE CUTS ACROSS HIS TAIL! MACHINE-GUN BULLETS SPLATTER THE SIDE OF HIS SOPWITH CAMEL! FLAMES! EXPLOSIONS! TERROR! OH, THE MEMORIES! THE FEAR!

SUDDENLY HE EMITS A TERRIBLE CRY OF ANGUISH....

AAUGHHH!

HERE'S THE WORLD WAR I PILOT BEING RETURNED TO HIS OUTFIT..
SCHULZ

HERE'S THE WORLD WAR I FLYING ACE IN PRISON..

A GUARD!

I LEAP ON THE GUARD, AND WRESTLE HIM TO THE GROUND! JUDO CHOP! WHAM! WHAM! WHAM!

I'M FREE! I'M FREE! I'M FREE!
NEVER STICK YOUR HEAD INTO AN EMPTY DOG HOUSE!
SCHULZ

HERE'S THE WORLD WAR I FLYING ACE ESCAPING IN A STOLEN FOKKER D7

WHAT'S THAT ? NIEUPORTS !! I'M BEING ATTACKED BY MY OWN BUDDIES!

HEY, IT'S ME! DON'T SHOOT! DON'T SHOOT!

GIVE MY REGARDS TO 'UNTER DEN LINDEN'!
SCHULZ

YOU KNOW WHAT I THINK?

I THINK YOU WOULD HAVE MADE A GOOD CAT!

NOT ME...

I COULD NEVER EAT A COLD MOUSE ON A FOGGY MORNING!
SCHULZ

JUST BEFORE HE TAKES OFF, THE WORLD WAR I FLYING ACE READS A LETTER FROM HOME..HIS GIRL HAS MARRIED HIS COUSIN WHO WORKS IN A SHIP YARD! WHAT A BITTER BLOW!

BROKEN-HEARTED, THE FLYING ACE CLIMBS INTO HIS SOPWITH CAMEL, AND TAKES OFF TO FLY OVER ENEMY LINES...
SNIF!
SNIF! SNIF!

BUT IT'S NO USE... HE HAS TO TURN AROUND...
SNIF!

HE CAN'T FLY WITH TEARS IN HIS EYES!
SCHULZ

SCHULZ

THIS CAN GET TO BE A DRAG...

I WISH YOU'D LEARN TO FIX YOUR OWN SUPPER

I WOULD, BUT I'M AFRAID I'D CUT MYSELF ON THE CAN OPENER!
SCHULZ

DIVING DOWN OUT OF THE CLOUDS I FIRE MY TWIN VICKERS AT THE RED BARON!

HE SWOOPS TO THE LEFT TO AVOID MY FIRE...I SWOOP RIGHT BEHIND HIM...HE SWOOPS TO THE RIGHT...

I SWOOP TO THE RIGHT...HE SWOOPS TO THE LEFT.... I SWOOP TO THE LEFT...HE SWOOPS TO THE RIGHT......I.....I.....I..

.....I FEEL SICK.......
SCHULZ

YOU THINK YOU'RE THE "ARM WRESTLING" CHAMP, DON'T YOU?

OF COURSE, I'M THE CHAMP... I'VE BEATEN EVERYBODY AROUND HERE!
NOT EVERYBODY...

YOU'RE NOT THE CHAMPION UNTIL YOU'VE BEATEN THE "MASKED MARVEL"......

OH, GOOD GRIEF!
SCHULZ

I REFUSE TO "ARM WRESTLE" WITH A STUPID BEAGLE!

I'LL BREAK HIS PAW OR HIS ARM OR HIS SHANK OR WHATEVER IT'S CALLED!

YOU'RE AFRAID OF THE "MASKED MARVEL"!
I'M NOT AFRAID! I JUST DON'T WANT TO BREAK HIS ARM OR WHATEVER IT IS!

I THINK IT'S A FRONT LEG..
SCHULZ

YOU STUPID DOG, COME BACK HERE WITH THAT SHOE!

DO YOU SEE THAT? HE'S GOT MY SHOE! THAT STUPID, NO-GOOD DOG OF YOURS HAS RUN OFF WITH MY SHOE!

COME BACK HERE WITH THAT SHOE, YOU STUPID DOG!!!

LOOK AT THIS...I'M WALKING AROUND WITH ONLY ONE SHOE! I CAN'T GO AROUND LIKE THIS...I'LL WEAR OUT MY SOCK!

WHAT ARE YOU GOING TO DO ABOUT IT?

WELL?

TICKLE! TICKLE! TICKLE!
SCHULZ

ALL RIGHT, YOU STUPID BEAGLE! YOU WANTED TO "ARM WRESTLE," LET'S "ARM WRESTLE"!

I'M GONNA SEND YOU BACK TO THE DOG POUND WHERE YOU BELONG, "MASKED MARVEL"!

I'M GONNA CLOBBER YOU! I'M GONNA RUN ROUGHSHOD OVER YOU! START PUSHING!

START? I'VE BEEN PUSHING FOR THREE MINUTES!
SCHULZ

HEY, C'MON! IT'S THE "ARM WRESTLING" CHAMPIONSHIP!

IT'S LUCY AGAINST THE "MASKED MARVEL"!

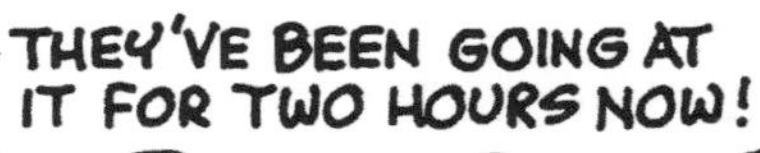
THEY'VE BEEN GOING AT IT FOR TWO HOURS NOW!

GIVE UP, YOU STUBBORN FEMALE!
CRACK, YOU STUPID BEAGLE!
SCHULZ

YIELD, YOU RASCAL!
SURRENDER, YOU DUMB DOG!

SUCCUMB, YOU DARK-HAIRED FIEND!
QUIT, YOU LONG-EARED MONSTER!

I CAN'T HOLD OUT ANOTHER SECOND...I'VE GOT TO DO SOMETHING!
I CAN'T HOLD OUT ANY LONGER! I THINK I'M GOING TO FAINT!

SMAK! AUGHH!
SCHULZ

IT WASN'T A FAIR FIGHT! HE KISSED ME!

HE KISSED ME WITH HIS STUPID DOG LIPS!!
BLEAH!

I'M STILL THE "ARM WRESTLING" CHAMP OF THE NEIGHBORHOOD!

YOU LET US DOWN, "MASKED MARVEL"
SORRY, BOYS...THAT'S THE WAY IT GOES....
SCHULZ

SUPPERTIME!

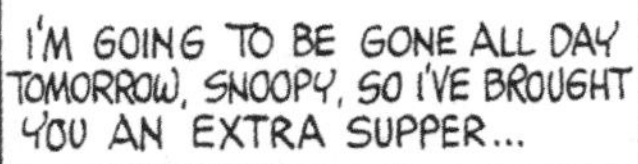
I'M GOING TO BE GONE ALL DAY TOMORROW, SNOOPY, SO I'VE BROUGHT YOU AN EXTRA SUPPER...

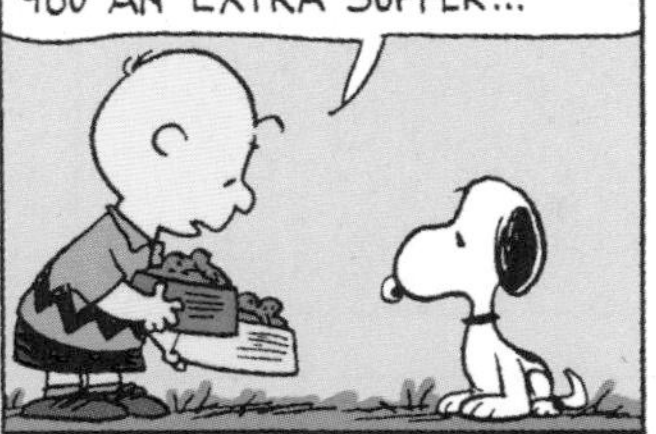

I'D ADVISE YOU NOT TO GET GREEDY, AND EAT IT BEFORE TOMORROW...

AAUGH!

I'M GLAD I ATE IT... I WOULD HAVE HATED MYSELF IF TOMORROW NEVER CAME!
SCHULZ

I WISH I WERE A PIRANHA FISH!

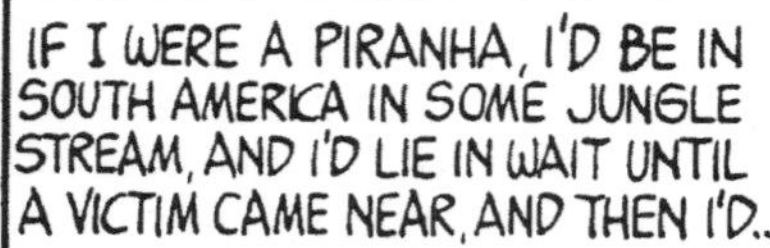
IF I WERE A PIRANHA, I'D BE IN SOUTH AMERICA IN SOME JUNGLE STREAM, AND I'D LIE IN WAIT UNTIL A VICTIM CAME NEAR, AND THEN I'D..

GRAB HIS LEG!!!...

WHAT HAPPENED TO YOUR SOCK?
WELL, I WAS CROSSING THIS JUNGLE STREAM IN SOUTH AMERICA, SEE, AND...
SCHULZ

MOM WANTS YOU TO RUN DOWN TO THE STORE FOR SOME BREAD

I CAN'T GO OUTSIDE... THERE'S A PIRANHA FISH WAITING OUT THERE TO CHOMP ME!

SEE?

IF YOU GET CHOMPED BY ONE OF US PIRANHA, BABY, YOU'VE HAD IT!
SCHULZ

I HEAR THERE'S A PIRANHA SWIMMING AROUND IN THE NEIGHBORHOOD...

BY GOLLY, THAT PIRANHA BETTER NOT TRY TO CHOMP ME!

ANY PIRANHA TRIES TO CHOMP ME, I'LL POUND HIM!!

THERE'S NOBODY AROUND HERE BUT US BEAGLES!
SCHULZ

!
flitter
flutter
flitter
flutter
flitter
flutter

whew!
GASP
GASP

Z
MUST HAVE BEEN A ROUGH FLIGHT
SCHULZ

HERE'S THE WORLD WAR I FLYING ACE WALKING OUT ONTO THE FIELD...

IT SNOWED LAST NIGHT... BUT TODAY THE SUN IS OUT.. THE SKY IS CLEAR..

I CLIMB INTO THE COCKPIT OF MY SOPWITH CAMEL...

"CHOCKS AWAY"

HERE'S THE WORLD WAR I FLYING ACE ZOOMING THROUGH THE AIR SEARCHING FOR THE RED BARON!

HE DOESN'T HAVE A CHANCE AGAINST MY SUPERIOR WEAPONS, TWO FIXED SYNCHRONISED VICKERS MACHINE GUNS MOUNTED ON TOP OF THE FUSELAGE AND FIRING THROUGH THE AIRSCREW ARC!

POW!

YOU'RE A POOR SPORT, RED BARON
SCHULZ

GRIPE
GRIPE
GRIPE
GRIPE

COMPLAIN
COMPLAIN
COMPLAIN
COMPLAIN
COMPLAIN

CRAB CRAB
CRAB CRAB
CRAB CRAB
CRAB CRAB

IF HE DOESN'T LIKE IT, WHY DOES HE KEEP FLYING DOWN THERE EVERY YEAR?
SCHULZ

flitter
flitter
flitter

I CAN'T FIGURE THAT GUY OUT...

HE'S EITHER A LOUSY FLYER OR HIS BLOOD SUGAR'S DOWN
SCHULZ

HERE'S THE WORLD WAR I PILOT WALKING OUT TO HIS SOPWITH CAMEL

WHERE'S MY MECHANIC? HOW CAN I FLY THIS PLANE WITHOUT MY MECHANIC?!

THEY DON'T CARE WHO THEY DRAFT THESE DAYS!
SCHULZ

"'ALL RIGHT,' SAID THE CAT; AND THIS TIME IT VANISHED QUITE SLOWLY...

BEGINNING WITH THE END OF THE TAIL, AND ENDING WITH THE GRIN, WHICH REMAINED SOME TIME AFTER THE REST OF IT HAD GONE."

I'VE BEEN ABLE TO DO THAT FOR YEARS!
SCHULZ

EXCUSE ME, SNOOPY, I HAVE TO GO EAT DINNER..
AND YOU HAVE TO WASH YOUR HANDS AGAIN BECAUSE YOU TOUCHED THE DOG!

OH, GOOD GRIEF!
"TOUCHED THE DOG"?!

"TOUCHED THE DOG"?!!
STAY AWAY FROM ME!! MY HANDS ARE CLEAN!

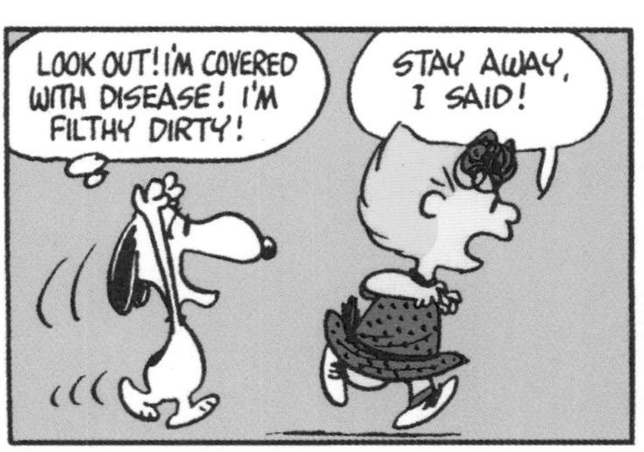
LOOK OUT! I'M COVERED WITH DISEASE! I'M FILTHY DIRTY!
STAY AWAY, I SAID!

HERE COMES THE BUBONIC PLAGUE! PAT MY HEAD AND GET A HANDFUL OF GERMS! HERE COMES THE WALKING DISEASE CARRIER! BEWARE! BEWARE!

LOOK OUT FOR ME...I'M DISEASED! I'M CONTAMINATED! I'M ...
HELP!

"TOUCHED THE DOG"! GOOD GRIEF!
SCHULZ

HAVE YOU EVER HEARD OF A CHESHIRE CAT?
SURE... IN "ALICE'S ADVENTURES IN WONDERLAND"

REMEMBER HOW SHE SAW THIS GRINNING CAT UP IN A TREE? AND REMEMBER HOW IT KEPT DISAPPEARING ALL THE TIME?

THE CAT DISAPPEARED LITTLE BY LITTLE UNTIL ONLY ITS GRIN WAS LEFT... I ALWAYS LIKED THAT PART...

IT'S A GREAT STORY, BUT IMPOSSIBLE, OF COURSE..
SCHULZ

"'WELL! I'VE OFTEN SEEN A CAT WITHOUT A GRIN,' THOUGHT ALICE.....
Alice's

'BUT A GRIN WITHOUT A CAT! IT'S THE MOST CURIOUS THING I EVER SAW IN ALL MY LIFE!'"
Alice's

Alice's

ACTUALLY, IT'S A CONDITIONED REFLEX!
Alice's
SCHULZ

HAVE YOU EVER SEEN A CHESHIRE BEAGLE ?

IF YOU PULL ANY OF THAT CHESHIRE-BEAGLE STUFF ON **ME** I'LL POUND YOU !!

RATS!

HOLD IT!!

IS THIS ALL YOU HAVE TO DO? ARE YOU GOING TO SPEND THE WHOLE DAY SLIDING BACK AND FORTH ON A PIECE OF ICE?!

DO YOU THINK THESE DAYS WERE GIVEN TO YOU TO WASTE? DOESN'T LIFE MEAN MORE TO YOU THAN THIS?!

SCHULZ

?

I DON'T MIND AS LONG AS THEY DON'T PLAY FOR MONEY..
SCHULZ

I THINK I'M WARPING!
SCHULZ

BOOT!

"THIS IS 'BE KIND TO ANIMALS WEEK'"
SCHULZ

HERE'S THE WORLD WAR I FLYING ACE ZOOMING THROUGH THE AIR IN HIS SOPWITH CAMEL

DOWN BELOW I CAN SEE THOSE POOR BLIGHTERS IN THE TRENCHES

SOMEDAY I SHOULD GO DOWN THERE...

I'VE ALWAYS WANTED TO MEET A BLIGHTER
SCHULZ

I'M HUNGRY!

ARE YOU OUT OF YOUR MIND? GO BACK TO SLEEP!

MY HEAD MAY GO TO SLEEP, BUT MY STOMACH WILL BE AWAKE ALL NIGHT!

ALL RIGHT, WAKE UP! YOU'RE THE ONE WHO WAS SO HUNGRY LAST NIGHT... HERE'S YOUR BREAKFAST!

RATS! NOW, MY HEAD'S AWAKE, BUT MY STOMACH'S ASLEEP!
SCHULZ

THIS IS "BE KIND TO ANIMALS WEEK"

THIS IS "BE KIND TO ANIMALS WEEK"

THIS IS "BE KIND TO ANIMALS WEEK"

NOT ON YOUR LIFE!

HERE'S THE WORLD WAR I FLYING ACE MAKING HIS WAY BACK TO THE AERODROME ACROSS NO-MAN'S LAND...

I FEEL SORRY FOR THE POOR BLIGHTERS WHO HAVE TO LIVE IN THESE TRENCHES...

OOPS! EXCUSE ME!

I TRIPPED OVER A BLIGHTER...

BEING A DOG IS NOT THE GREATEST THING IN THE WORLD

WE HAVE A LOT OF DISADVANTAGES..

WHAT I'M TRYING TO SAY IS.... LIFE IS HARD ENOUGH...

WHY RAIN ON ME?!
SCHULZ

HERE'S THE WORLD WAR I PILOT SITTING ON HIS BUNK WRITING TO HIS GIRL BACK HOME

" DEAR SWEETIE, IT HAS BEEN RAINING HERE LATELY, BUT ALL GOES WELL "

"GENERAL PERSHING HAS ASKED FOR MY ADVICE SEVERAL TIMES... I ALWAYS TRY TO HELP HIM OUT"

ACTUALLY, I'VE NEVER EVEN MET GENERAL PERSHING!
SCHULZ

HERE'S THE WORLD WAR I FLYING ACE TAKING OFF IN HIS SOPWITH CAMEL

AS I PASS OVER THE FRONT LINES, I CAN SEE BURSTS OF ARTILLERY FIRE BELOW ME...

GREAT SCOTT! AN ENEMY OBSERVATION BALLOON!

THE WINGS ON MY PLANE SHRIEK IN PROTEST AS I TURN SHARPLY TO GET INTO POSITION...

GOOD GRIEF! MY GUNS ARE JAMMED!

I CAN'T LET THAT BALLOON GET AWAY...

AS MY PLANE DIVES PAST THE BALLOON, I LEAP OUT AT THE OBSERVER!

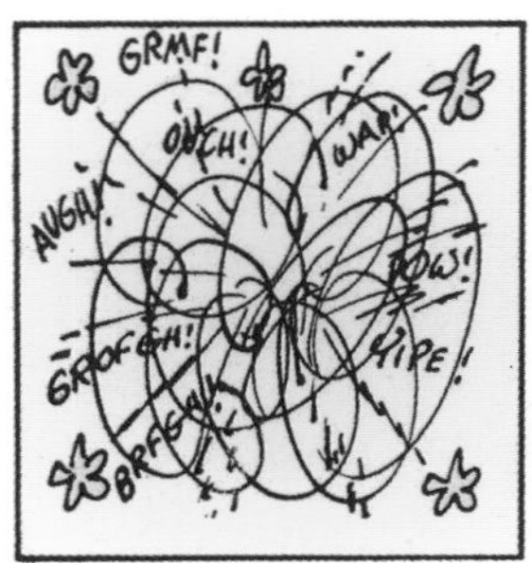
GRMF!
OUCH!
WAP!
AUGH!
POW!
GROFGH!
YIPE!

SOME OF THOSE BALLOON OBSERVERS ARE PRETTY TOUGH...
SCHULZ

!

I CAN SEE MYSELF IN MY WATER DISH..

I HAVE A CUTE SMILE!
SCHULZ

WELL, SCHOOL'S OVER, AND HERE I AM IN A BUS GOING TO SUMMER CAMP..

SIGH

AT LEAST THIS YEAR I'M NOT HAVING TO GO ALONE...

HERE'S THE WORLD WAR I FLYING ACE RIDING ACROSS FRANCE ON A TROOP TRAIN...
SCHULZ

NOT "LUNCH"... CHOW! WE WORLD WAR I FLYING ACES ALWAYS CALL IT "CHOW"... WHAT A MISERABLE CAMP.. WE MUST BE FIFTY KILOMETERS FROM THE NEAREST VILLAGE! CURSE THIS HOT WEATHER! CURSE THIS STUPID WAR!

I WONDER WHAT WE...
THERE'S A BUG IN YOUR HAIR, CHARLIE BROWN...

WHERE? WHERE? BRUSH IT OFF!
THAT'S ALL RIGHT... IT'S GONE NOW...

THAT'S THE ONE THING I HATE ABOUT ALL THIS OUTDOOR LIVING!
WELL, DON'T WORRY...IT'S NOT IN YOUR HAIR ANY MORE..

IT FELL DOWN YOUR NECK!
SCHULZ

YOU STILL HAVEN'T TOLD ME WHAT YOU'RE DOING HERE
THE GIRLS' CAMP IS GOING TO PLAY THE BOYS' CAMP IN A BALL GAME...AREN'T YOU GOING TO PLAY?

THEY HAVEN'T ASKED ME...I DON'T THINK I'M GOOD ENOUGH..
BUT YOU LOVE BASEBALL, CHARLIE BROWN..

THIS IS A SUMMER CAMP! YOU'RE HERE TO HAVE FUN NO MATTER HOW LOUSY YOU ARE! I'LL GO SPEAK TO YOUR COUNSELOR, CHARLIE BROWN...

SO LONG, SWEETIE...
POOR, UNFORTUNATE GIRL...SHE MUST BE STARVED FOR LOVE... CURSE THIS WAR!
SMAK
SCHULZ

CLOMP!

ALL RIGHT, I SAW THAT! BUT I'M GOING TO PRETEND THAT IT NEVER HAPPENED!

I'M NOT GOING TO MOVE! I'M NOT GOING TO CHASE YOU! IF YOU BRING THAT BALL BACK HERE BEFORE I COUNT TO TEN, WE'LL JUST PRETEND THAT NOTHING HAPPENED!

ONE, TWO, THREE, FOUR, FIVE, SIX, SEVEN, EIGHT, NINE...

THANK YOU...THAT WAS A VERY WISE DECISION!
PFFT!

SIGH
SCHULZ

DEAR MOM AND DAD,
SNOOPY AND I ARRIVED AT CAMP YESTERDAY.

WE ARE HAVING A GOOD TIME. PEPPERMINT PATTY IS HERE, AND IS GOING TO GET ME ON THE BALL TEAM.

I HOPE YOU LIKE THIS POST CARD. PLEASE GREET SALLY FOR ME.

DO YOU HAVE ANYTHING SPECIAL YOU'D LIKE TO SAY?
GIVE MY REGARDS TO BROADWAY!
SCHULZ

STRIKE THREE!

"HEY, KID, WHO TOLD YOU YOU WERE A BALL PLAYER?"
BOO!! BOO!!
"GET OFF THE FIELD, KID!"
"WE CAN DO WITHOUT YOUR KIND, KID!"

"WHERE'D YOU LEARN TO PLAY BALL, KID, IN KINDERGARTEN?!!!"
HA!HA! HA!HA! HA!HA!
HA!HA! HA!HA! HA!HA!

SPRING LAKE
summer camp
FUN! RECREATION!
COMPANIONSHIP!
SIGH
SCHULZ

HI, CHUCK... GREAT GAME YESTERDAY, WASN'T IT?

BEAUTIFUL!
SORRY I HAD TO STRIKE YOU OUT

FOR A WHILE I CONSIDERED LETTING YOU HIT ONE AND BE A HERO, BUT I KNEW YOU WOULDN'T WANT ME TO DO THAT...

OH?
SCHULZ

HERE'S THE WORLD WAR I FLYING ACE STANDING OUT UNDER THE STARS...IT'S A BEAUTIFUL NIGHT...

SOMEWHERE OFF IN THE DISTANCE IS THE LOW RUMBLE OF ARTILLERY FIRE.. AS HE LOOKS AT THE SKY, HE THINKS OF THE PEOPLE AT HOME, AND WONDERS IF THEY'RE LOOKING AT THE SAME SKY... AND THEN HE IS SAD...

SLOWLY HE WALKS BACK ACROSS THE DARKENED AERODROME, AND THEN THE THOUGHT THAT THROBS SO CONSTANTLY IN HIS MIND CRIES OUT..

CURSE YOU, RED BARON!
SCHULZ

HEY, CHARLIE BROWN, COME QUICK! THEY'RE HAVING A CANOE RACE!

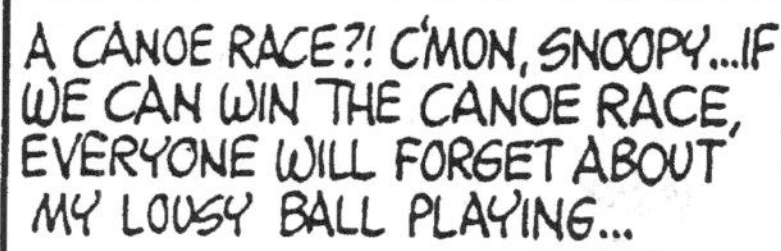
A CANOE RACE?! C'MON, SNOOPY...IF WE CAN WIN THE CANOE RACE, EVERYONE WILL FORGET ABOUT MY LOUSY BALL PLAYING...

WE'LL SHOW 'EM, SNOOPY...WE'LL GET IN THIS CANOE, WE'LL WIN THIS RACE AND WE'LL BE HEROES!

ACTUALLY, I HAD PLANNED FOR YOU TO HELP WITH THE PADDLING..
SCHULZ

WE'RE GONNA WIN THIS CANOE RACE, SNOOPY, OR DIE TRYING! I'M GONNA PADDLE AN' PADDLE AN'...

WHEW I'M EXHAUSTED! I FEEL LIKE I'VE PADDLED A HUNDRED MILES......

I WONDER IF WE WON...

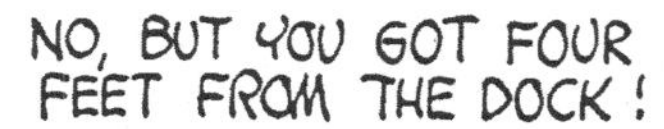
NO, BUT YOU GOT FOUR FEET FROM THE DOCK!

SCHULZ

HERE'S THE WORLD WAR I PILOT STANDING IN A LINE OF CAPTURED PRISONERS...
ONE, PLEASE

WE ARE ABOUT TO BE QUESTIONED BY THE INTERROGATING OFFICER...I WON'T TELL THEM A THING...IN FACT, MY MIND IS RACING WITH PLANS TO ESCAPE....
ONE, PLEASE

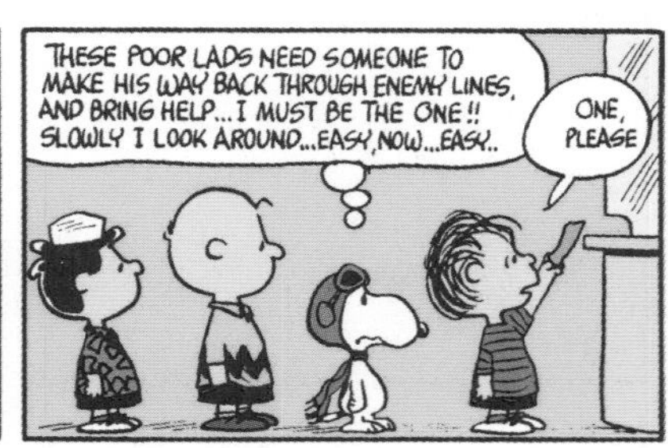
THESE POOR LADS NEED SOMEONE TO MAKE HIS WAY BACK THROUGH ENEMY LINES, AND BRING HELP...I MUST BE THE ONE!! SLOWLY I LOOK AROUND...EASY, NOW...EASY..
ONE, PLEASE

SUDDENLY I MAKE MY BREAK!

ONE, PLEASE

PARDON ME?

OH, HIM...THE LITTLE KID WITH THE GOGGLES? WHERE WAS HE GOING?

WELL, MA'AM...IT WOULD BE A LONG STORY, AND I DOUBT IF YOU'D BELIEVE IT EVEN IF I TOLD YOU... ONE, PLEASE
SCHULZ

FROM CAMP! I'M BACK FROM SUMMER CAMP... I WAS AWAY FOR TWO WEEKS TO SUMMER CAMP, AND NOW I'M BACK!

GROWF!

I HATE BEING STARED AT!
SCHULZ

YOU DOGS NEVER CONTRIBUTE! YOU NEVER **DO** ANYTHING!

JUST ASK YOURSELF...WHAT HAVE I DONE FOR MANKIND?

WELL, I HAVEN'T BITTEN ANYONE ON THE LEG LATELY.....

IT'S KIND OF NEGATIVE, BUT IT'S SOMETHING!
SCHULZ

LOOK AT THAT STUPID BIRD, WILL YOU?

HE THINKS HE'S GOING TO BUILD A NEST ON TOP OF MY STOMACH...

THE NERVE OF HIM! THE UNMITIGATED GALL! HIM AND HIS TWIGS AND STRING...

BY GOLLY, I'M GOING TO FIX HIS WAGON!

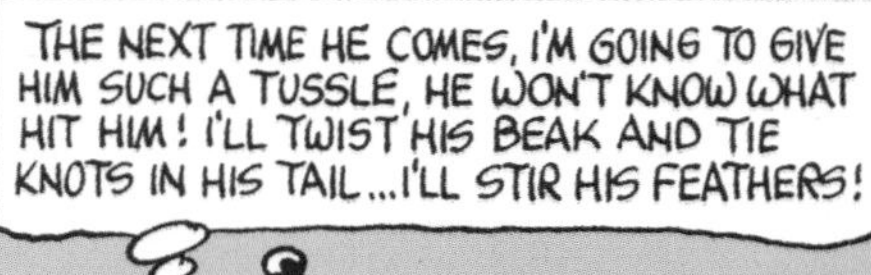
THE NEXT TIME HE COMES, I'M GOING TO GIVE HIM SUCH A TUSSLE, HE WON'T KNOW WHAT HIT HIM! I'LL TWIST HIS BEAK AND TIE KNOTS IN HIS TAIL...I'LL STIR HIS FEATHERS!

GET READY, BIRD! THIS IS IT!

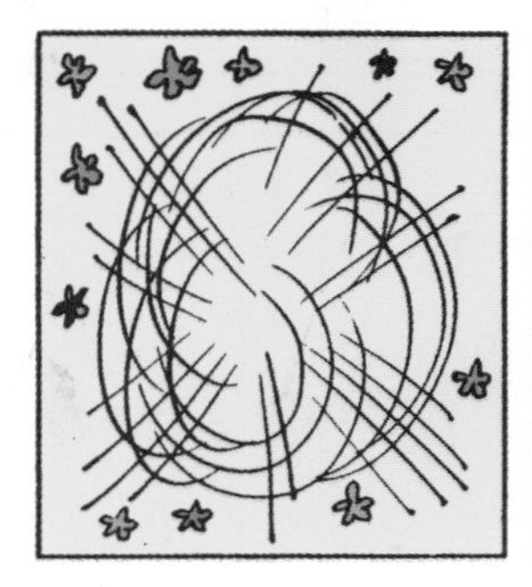

I CAN'T STAND IT!
SCHULZ

HERE'S THE WORLD WAR I FLYING ACE ABOUT TO TAKE OFF IN HIS SOPWITH CAMEL

"CONTACT!" HE SHOUTS...

?

I SEE MY MECHANIC HAS SPENT THE WEEK-END IN PARIS AGAIN
Z
SCHULZ

DO YOU SEE THIS STICK?

I, THE HUMAN BEING, WILL THROW THE STICK, AND YOU, THE DOG, WILL RETRIEVE IT!

I, THE DOG, COULD NOT BE LESS INTERESTED!
SCHULZ

YESTERDAY, I THREW THIS STICK, BUT YOU FAILED TO RETRIEVE IT..

I, THE HUMAN BEING, IN OUR GREAT TRADITION OF FORGIVENESS, WILL GIVE YOU, THE DOG, A SECOND CHANCE..

I, THE DOG, THANK YOU FOR THIS SECOND CHANCE...

BUT FORGET IT!!
SCHULZ

HI, SWEETIE!

ACTUALLY, VULTURES JUST **HATE** TO BE CALLED "SWEETIE"!
SCHULZ

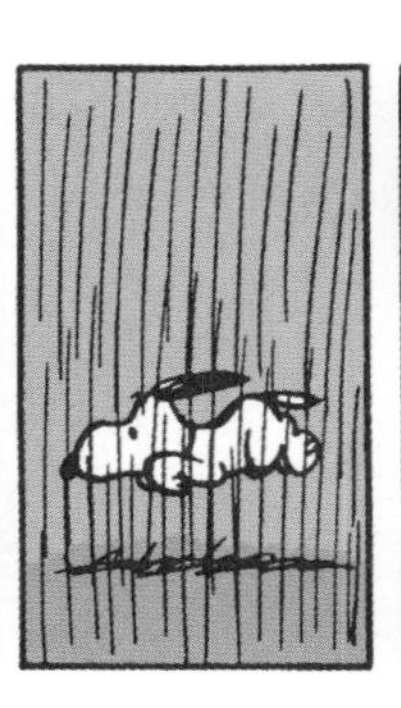

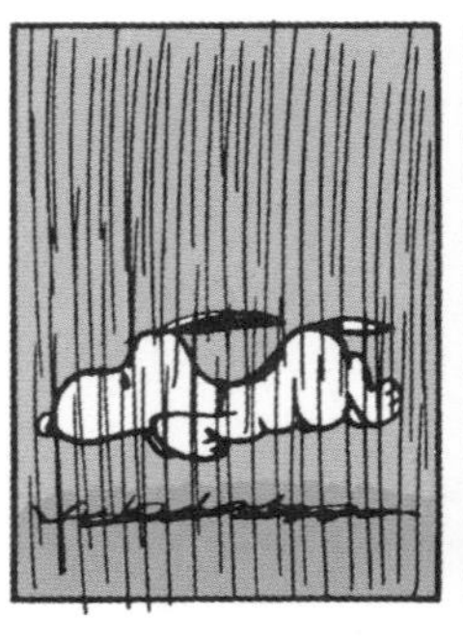

RAP! RAP! RAP!
RAP! RAP!

NOW I'M WIDE AWAKE, AND MY WHOLE ROOM SMELLS LIKE A WET DOG!

I'M GLAD I'M NOT A BUG.... BUGS HAVE A TERRIBLE LIFE..

I'M SURE THAT THIS BUG WISHES HE WERE ME...

SIGH

I KNEW IT... THAT WAS A SIGH OF ENVY!
SCHULZ

SAY, THERE'S A CUTE LITTLE BUG...

I WONDER WHY SHE'S SO MUCH CUTER THAN OTHER BUGS?

SHE'S WEARING EYE-SHADOW!
SCHULZ

HERE'S THE VULTURE PERCHED HIGH IN A TREE...

IF A VICTIM COMES AROUND, HE'LL SWOOP DOWN ON HIM!

YES, SIR! IT'LL BE, "GET READY, GET SET, GO!!"

ACTUALLY, REAL VULTURES ALMOST NEVER SAY, "GET READY, GET SET, GO!!"
SCHULZ

THAT DIDN'T REALLY BOTHER ME...IF YOU EXPECT NOTHING, YOU GET NOTHING...
SCHULZ

BRING YOUR ROOT BEER IN HERE, CHARLIE BROWN..WE'LL SIT AND WATCH TV
SNIF?

YOU SNIFFED IN MY ROOT BEER!

YOUR STUPID DOG SNIFFED IN MY ROOT BEER!!

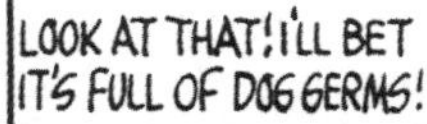

LOOK AT THAT! I'LL BET IT'S FULL OF DOG GERMS!

WHERE'S MY BINOCULARS?
BINOCULARS?

AH, HA! I THOUGHT SO!

SEE? I POURED A LITTLE ROOT BEER IN THIS SAUCER AND EXAMINED IT WITH MY BINOCULARS... IT'S FULL OF DOG GERMS!

I GUESS THAT WHOLE BUSINESS WAS MY FAULT, SNOOPY... I'VE NEVER DISCUSSED ETIQUETTE WITH YOU...

THERE'S ONE THING YOU SHOULD NEVER DO...NEVER SNIFF IN YOUR HOSTESS'S ROOT BEER!

I'LL REMEMBER THAT...

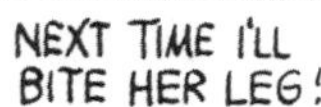

NEXT TIME I'LL BITE HER LEG!
SCHULZ

HERE'S THE WORLD WAR I FLYING ACE ZOOMING THROUGH THE AIR SEARCHING FOR THE RED BARON..

MY RIGHT HAND IS ON THE SPADE-GRIP STICK WITH MY THUMB OVER THE GUN TRIGGERS...MY LEFT HAND IS ON THE BENTLEY ROTARY THROTTLE

RATS!

MY RESEARCH IS GOOD, BUT MY FLYING IS LOUSY!
SCHULZ

GET YOUR PAW OFF MY BLANKET, YOU STUPID DOG, OR BE PREPARED TO SUFFER THE CONSEQUENCES!

SIGH

MY LIFE IS FULL OF UNSUFFERED CONSEQUENCES...
SCHULZ

HERE'S THE FIERCE VULTURE WAITING PATIENTLY FOR A VICTIM...

WAITING...WAITING...WAITING..

WAITING....

SCHULZ
YOU CAN'T POSSIBLY REALIZE HOW ANNOYING THAT IS!

SORRY, NO DOGS ALLOWED IN THIS POOL!

SURELY YOU CAN'T MEAN **ME** ?!
SCHULZ

HERE'S THE FIERCE LEOPARD HIDING IN A TREE WAITING FOR A VICTIM TO COME ALONG!

I HEAR FOOTSTEPS, BUT I CAN'T SEE ANYTHING!

STUPID TREE!

RATS!
SCHULZ

AND HOW ABOUT THOSE TWO? GOSH, THAT SEEMS LIKE A LONG TIME AGO... ⁂ SIGH ⁂

SEPTEMBER RAINS MAKE ME LONESOME!
SCHULZ

YOU SHOULDN'T JUST LIE AROUND ALL DAY...

ON THE WAY OVER HERE, I SAW TWO DOGS WRESTLING AROUND AND HAVING A GREAT TIME...THEY WERE CHASING EACH OTHER, LEAPING IN THE AIR, ROLLING ON THE GROUND....

THAT'S WHAT YOU SHOULD DO...GET OUT AND PLAY WITH YOUR OWN KIND..

I WOULD, BUT I HATE GETTING COVERED WITH A LOT OF DOG HAIR!
SCHULZ

HEE! HEE! HEE! HEE!

?

CHUCKLE CHUCKLE CHUCKLE

HEE HEE HEE HEE
HEE HEE HEE HEE HEE

CHUCKLE CHUCKLE CHUCKLE

HOW CAN ANYONE SIT AROUND BY HIMSELF LAUGHING AND DRAWING INSULTING PICTURES OF CATS?

WHEN YOU LIVE ALONE, YOU LEARN TO AMUSE YOURSELF!
SCHULZ

NO AFTER-DINNER SPEAKER?
SCHULZ

SORRY, SNOOPY...THE NEW RULE SAYS, "NO DOGS ALLOWED ON SCHOOL PLAYGROUND"

IT'S THEIR LOSS, NOT MINE!
SCHULZ

THIS IS NATIONAL DOG WEEK

GET OUT OF HERE!
SCHULZ

THIS IS NATIONAL DOG WEEK

I'M WELL AWARE OF THAT, BUT WHAT CAN A PERSON DO TO MAKE IT MEANINGFUL?

HUG A BEAGLE!

NOW YOU KNOW!
SCHULZ

BEAUTIFUL, ISN'T IT?
YES, BUT SOMETHING SEEMS STRANGE...

"WHEN THE EARTH WAS YOUNG AND THE MOON WAS FIRST FORMED, THE MOON WAS ONLY ABOUT 15,000 MILES FROM THE EARTH."

"OVER A PERIOD OF MILLIONS OF YEARS THE MOON HAS BEEN MOVING AWAY FROM THE EARTH AT A RATE OF ABOUT FIVE FEET EVERY ONE HUNDRED YEARS."

I THOUGHT IT LOOKED A LITTLE FARTHER AWAY THAN BEFORE..
SCHULZ

HERE'S THE FIERCE MOUNTAIN LION SITTING ON A ROCK WAITING FOR A VICTIM TO COME ALONG..

YOU THINK YOU LOOK LIKE A FIERCE MOUNTAIN LION SITTING ON A ROCK WAITING FOR A VICTIM TO COME ALONG, DON'T YOU?

WELL, YOU DON'T! YOU LOOK LIKE A STUPID BEAGLE SITTING ON A ROCK PRETENDING HE'S A FIERCE MOUNTAIN LION SITTING ON A ROCK WAITING FOR A VICTIM TO COME ALONG!

I HAD A HARD TIME FOLLOWING THAT...
SCHULZ

IF IT BITES ME, I'LL SCREAM!
SCHULZ

HEADING SOUTH FOR THE WINTER, EH? WELL, ENJOY YOURSELF!

I KNEW HE WAS GOING THE WRONG WAY, BUT I DIDN'T SAY ANYTHING!
SCHULZ

I KNEW I SHOULDN'T HAVE DONE IT...

I FETCHED THAT STUPID TENNIS BALL FOR THOSE KIDS ALL AFTERNOON..

SO WHAT HAPPENS WHEN I WAKE UP FROM MY NAP?

"TENNIS BALL MOUTH"!
BLEAH!
SCHULZ

WELL?!

OH, ALL RIGHT!

I MUST BE OUT OF MY MIND!

SCHULZ
SO WHAT'S WRONG WITH WANTING TO BE SERVED ON A TEA CART?

THANK YOU FOR THE DANCE!
SCHULZ

SOME PEOPLE DON'T APPROVE OF DANCING

DON'T YOU REALIZE THAT YOU MAY BE OFFENDING SOMEONE?

ME? ME OFFENDING SOMEONE? SWEET, INNOCENT, LITTLE OL' ME?

HEE HEE HEE HEE HEE HEE
SIGH
SCHULZ

HERE'S THE WORLD WAR I FLYING ACE GOING INTO A LITTLE FRENCH CAFE NEAR APREMONT...

GARÇON! A ROOT BEER, PLEASE! WHY IS IT SO QUIET IN HERE? LET'S HAVE A LITTLE MUSIC!

WOULD MADEMOISELLE CARE TO DANCE? AH, SHE CANNOT RESIST THE CHARMS OF THE HANDSOME PILOT OF THE ALLIES...

"IT'S A LONG WAY TO TIPPERARY..."

GARÇON! MORE ROOT BEER! ROOT BEER FOR EVERYONE!
WHEEEEE!!

VIVE LA FRANCE! VIVENT LES AMERICAINS!

CURSE THIS STUPID WAR!

WELL, LADS, THAT'S ENOUGH FOR TONIGHT... WE MUSTN'T FORGET THAT WE HAVE A JOB OF WORK TO DO!

THE SUN IS JUST COMING UP AS I REACH THE AERODROME..

HERE'S THE WORLD WAR I FLYING ACE TAKING OFF WITH THE DAWN PATROL...

SUDDENLY A RED FOKKER TRIPLANE APPEARS IN THE SKY!!

THE RED BARON IS SMART.. HE NEVER SPENDS THE WHOLE NIGHT DANCING AND DRINKING ROOT BEER..
SCHULZ

YOU'VE BEEN DANCING ALMOST ALL DAY...

IF YOU KNEW HOW MUCH SADNESS THERE IS IN THIS WORLD, YOU WOULDN'T BE DANCING!

I'M GLAD YOU CAME TO YOUR SENSES..

IT WASN'T THAT...MY FEET WERE BEGINNING TO HURT!
SCHULZ

BIRDS THINK I HAVE A NICE FACE!
SCHULZ

"WE THANK YOU FOR SUBMITTING YOUR MATERIAL..HOWEVER, WE REGRET THAT IT DOES NOT SUIT OUR PRESENT NEEDS"

SCHULZ

THIS IS MY INDIAN SUMMER DANCE..

ACTUALLY, I'M NEVER QUITE SURE JUST WHEN INDIAN SUMMER IS...SOME SAY IT'S THE WARM DAYS THAT FOLLOW THE FIRST FROST OF LATE AUTUMN..

I DON'T KNOW..MAYBE INDIAN SUMMER IS OVER... MAYBE IT NEVER CAME...

ANYWAY, IT'S A NICE DAY, AND JUST IN CASE THIS IS INDIAN SUMMER, THIS IS MY INDIAN SUMMER DANCE!
SCHULZ

CLOMP!

COME BACK HERE WITH THAT BLANKET, YOU CRAZY DOG!

NOW, WHERE DID HE GO?
HEE HEE HEE HEE

I CAN'T IMAGINE WHERE HE WENT...

IT'S PRETTY HOT OUT HERE TODAY... THAT OL' SUN IS REALLY BEATING DOWN..

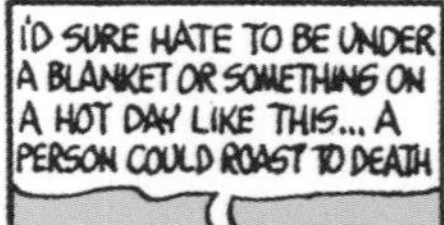
I'D SURE HATE TO BE UNDER A BLANKET OR SOMETHING ON A HOT DAY LIKE THIS... A PERSON COULD ROAST TO DEATH

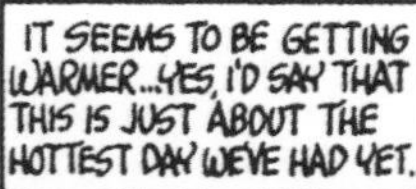
IT SEEMS TO BE GETTING WARMER...YES, I'D SAY THAT THIS IS JUST ABOUT THE HOTTEST DAY WE'VE HAD YET..

GASP!

THIS DESERT'S TOO BIG TO CROSS AT NOON, BOYS... LET'S WAIT 'TIL THE COOL OF EVENING..
STUPID DOG!
SCHULZ

TRICKS OR TREATS!

BAM!
BAM!
BAM!

WHO WAS IT THIS TIME, DEAR?
CHOMP CHOMP CHOMP
I COULDN'T TELL.. SOME LITTLE KID IN A DOG COSTUME
SCHULZ

SNOOPY, I HAVE GREAT NEWS FOR YOU...

I AM GOING TO LET YOU SIT IN THE PUMPKIN PATCH WITH ME THIS YEAR, AND WAIT FOR THE ARRIVAL OF THE "GREAT PUMPKIN"!

HMM...TO QUOTE A WELL-WORN AND TIME-HONORED PHRASE...

"THRILLSVILLE!"
SCHULZ

ON HALLOWEEN NIGHT THE "GREAT PUMPKIN" RISES OUT OF THE PUMPKIN PATCH THAT HE PICKS AS THE MOST SINCERE

THEN HE FLIES THROUGH THE AIR BRINGING TOYS TO ALL THE GOOD CHILDREN IN THE WORLD!

JUST THINK, SNOOPY, IF HE PICKS THIS PUMPKIN PATCH, YOU AND I WILL BE HERE TO SEE HIM!

FRANKLY, THIS LOOKS LIKE A GOOD PLACE TO GET MUGGED!
SCHULZ

I WISH YOU COULD TALK, SNOOPY...

HERE YOU ARE SITTING IN A PUMPKIN PATCH WITH THE POSSIBILITY OF SEEING THE "GREAT PUMPKIN"... IT'S AN EMOTIONAL EXPERIENCE..

I'D REALLY BE INTERESTED IN KNOWING WHAT THOUGHTS ARE RUNNING THROUGH YOUR MIND...

WHEN DO WE EAT?
SCHULZ

WHAT ARE YOU GUYS DOING?
WE'RE WAITING FOR THE "GREAT PUMPKIN"

IF HE SELECTS THIS PUMPKIN PATCH AS THE MOST SINCERE, WE'LL GET TO SEE HIM!
OH, BROTHER..

I THINK YOU'RE BOTH CRAZY!
WE DON'T CARE WHAT YOU THINK, DO WE, SNOOPY?

SCHULZ

HALLOWEEN WILL SOON BE HERE..

AND WHAT AM I DOING? I'M SITTING IN A PUMPKIN PATCH WITH THIS STUPID KID WAITING FOR THE "GREAT PUMPKIN"

WHY?

THE ONLY CONCLUSION I CAN COME TO IS THAT I REPRESENT A DECLINE IN BEAGLE MENTALITY!
SCHULZ

THIS IS IT, SNOOPY..THIS IS HALLOWEEN NIGHT...

IF THE "GREAT PUMPKIN" PICKS THIS PUMPKIN PATCH AS THE MOST SINCERE, WE'LL GET TO SEE HIM! NOW, I...

WHAT'S THAT?
WHAT'S WHAT?

RUSTLE
RUSTLE
RUSTLE
IT'S THE "GREAT PUMPKIN"! HE'S RISING OUT OF THE PUMPKIN PATCH!
I NEVER SHOULD HAVE LEFT THE DAISY HILL PUPPY FARM!
SCHULZ

I CAN'T BELIEVE IT... WHAT A DISAPPOINTMENT!

I APOLOGIZE, SNOOPY... WHEN I HEARD ALL THAT RUSTLING IN THE PUMPKIN PATCH, I THOUGHT FOR SURE IT WAS THE "GREAT PUMPKIN"

AND WHO DOES IT TURN OUT TO BE?

A BIRD-HIPPIE!
SCHULZ

I'VE BEEN GOING OVER OUR BASEBALL STATISTICS FOR THIS PAST YEAR..

WHEN I THINK OF ALL THOSE GAMES WE LOST, I GET SICK..

WINNING ISN'T EVERYTHING, CHARLIE BROWN...

THAT'S TRUE, BUT LOSING ISN'T **ANYTHING**!
SCHULZ

NO! ABSOLUTELY NOT!!

WHY CAN'T YOU EAT YOUR SUPPER LIKE ANY NORMAL DOG? WHO DO YOU THINK YOU ARE?!

OH, ALL RIGHT!

I GIVE UP! I'M SO WISHY-WASHY IT'S SICKENING!

SUPPERTIME!

I'VE ALWAYS WANTED TO EAT IN A CAFETERIA...MMM! EVERYTHING LOOKS SO GOOD... I'LL HAVE SOME OF THIS AND SOME OF THAT..SOME OF THIS AND...
I CAN'T STAND IT!
SCHULZ

LAST YEAR WAS THE WORST BASEBALL SEASON OUR TEAM HAS HAD YET!

I'M REALLY WORRIED ABOUT OUR TEAM, SCHROEDER... I THINK WE'RE GETTING WORSE..

BEETHOVEN HAD HIS PROBLEMS, TOO!

THAT'S WHAT I LIKE, A NICE RELEVANT STATEMENT..
SCHULZ

I'VE MADE A BIG DECISION...

THIS IS THE TIME OF YEAR WHEN ALL THE BIG BASEBALL TRADES ARE MADE...I'M GOING TO TRY TO IMPROVE OUR TEAM WITH A FEW SHREWD TRADES

THAT'S A GREAT IDEA, CHARLIE BROWN...

WHY DON'T YOU TRADE YOURSELF?
SCHULZ

HELLO, PEPPERMINT PATTY? I WAS WONDERING IF YOU'D BE INTERESTED IN TRADING A FEW BASEBALL PLAYERS..

WELL, I DON'T KNOW, CHUCK...THE ONLY GOOD PLAYER YOU HAVE IS THAT LITTLE KID WITH THE BIG NOSE

YOU MEAN, SNOOPY? OH, NO, I COULD NEVER TRADE HIM... I WAS THINKING MORE OF LUCY...

HELLO? HELLO?
SCHULZ

HOW ARE YOUR BASEBALL TRADES COMING, CHARLIE BROWN?

TERRIBLE..PEPPERMINT PATTY SAID THE ONLY PLAYER SHE'D BE INTERESTED IN WOULD BE SNOOPY...

I TOLD HER, "NO"....BUT MAYBE I WAS WRONG...
YOU MEAN YOU'D TRADE YOUR OWN DOG JUST TO WIN A FEW BALL GAMES?!

"WIN"....HAVE YOU EVER NOTICED WHAT A BEAUTIFUL WORD THAT IS? "WIN!" WHAT A WONDERFUL SOUND! "WIN!" "WIN!" "WIN!"
SCHULZ

HERE'S THE FIERCE VULTURE SITTING HIGH IN A TREE WAITING FOR A VICTIM TO COME ALONG..

AH! A VICTIM APPROACHES! AS HE PASSES BY THE TREE, I SHALL SWOOP DOWN UPON HIM!

GET READY.... GET SET....

SWOOP!

KLUNK!

IF YOU'LL PARDON MY SAYING SO, YOUR "SWOOPING" LEAVES MUCH TO BE DESIRED...

MAYBE I COULD GO TO SWOOP SCHOOL...
SCHULZ

HELLO, PEPPERMINT PATTY? I'VE DECIDED TO TAKE YOU UP ON YOUR OFFER..

THAT'S GREAT, CHUCK...I'LL GIVE YOU FIVE PLAYERS FOR SNOOPY... I GUARANTEE IT'LL IMPROVE YOUR TEAM..WHY DON'T I BRING A CONTRACT OVER ON MONDAY, AND WE'LL SETTLE THE WHOLE DEAL, OKAY?

UH...YEAH...OKAY... OKAY...FINE..FINE.....
GOODBY...

WHAT HAVE I DONE? I'VE TRADED AWAY MY OWN DOG! I'VE BECOME A REAL MANAGER!!
SCHULZ

OKAY, CHUCK..HERE'S THE CONTRACT... I'M TRADING YOU FIVE PLAYERS FOR SNOOPY...

I'M KIND OF NERVOUS...I'VE NEVER TAKEN PART IN ANY BIG BASEBALL TRADES BEFORE...MAYBE I SHOULD THINK ABOUT THIS A LITTLE WHILE, AND..

DON'T BE RIDICULOUS...YOU WANT TO BUILD A BETTER TEAM, DON'T YOU? COME ON, SIGN RIGHT HERE..

TRY NOT TO LET YOUR HAND SHAKE SO MUCH, CHUCK, YOU'RE SPILLING INK ALL OVER THE CONTRACT
SCHULZ

SNOOPY, THIS IS A HARD THING FOR ME TO SAY..

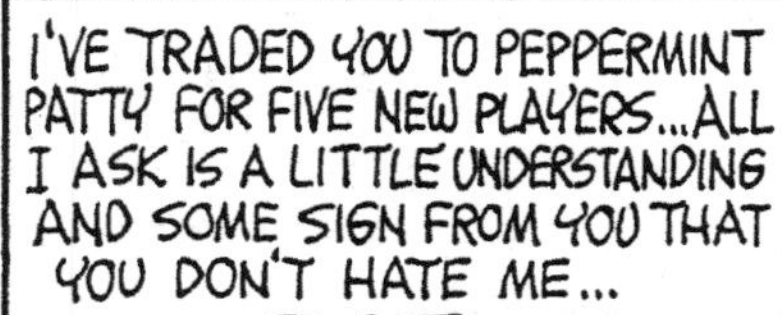
I'VE TRADED YOU TO PEPPERMINT PATTY FOR FIVE NEW PLAYERS...ALL I ASK IS A LITTLE UNDERSTANDING AND SOME SIGN FROM YOU THAT YOU DON'T HATE ME...

BLEAH!!

THAT WASN'T IT!
SCHULZ

YOU WHAT?!!

I TRADED SNOOPY TO PEPPERMINT PATTY FOR FIVE GOOD PLAYERS... HE'S THE ONLY PLAYER SHE'D TRADE FOR... I HAD TO DO IT...

BUT HE'S YOUR OWN DOG! DOES WINNING A BALL GAME MEAN THAT MUCH TO YOU?

I DON'T KNOW...I'VE NEVER WON A BALL GAME...
SCHULZ

I HOPE YOU ENJOYED YOUR SUPPER.. WE WERE OUT OF DOG FOOD SO I BORROWED SOME CAT FOOD FROM THE PEOPLE NEXT DOOR...

CAT FOOD?

I FEEL SICK!

MY STOMACH HURTS..

I THINK I'M DYING...

WHAT A DUMB THING TO DO...FEED A SENSITIVE DOG SOME CAT FOOD! I CAN'T BELIEVE IT... OOOO! WHAT PAIN!!

THOSE STUPID CATS CAN STAND STUFF LIKE THAT BECAUSE THEY'RE ALWAYS EATING RAW MICE AND STUPID THINGS LIKE THAT, BUT WE DOGS ARE..

ACTUALLY, I WAS KIDDING YOU...IT WASN'T CAT FOOD AT ALL...IT WAS THE SAME THING YOU EAT EVERY NIGHT!

I'D BITE HIM ON THE LEG, BUT MY STOMACH FEELS TOO GOOD..
SCHULZ

I'M A GREAT BELIEVER IN WINTER CONDITIONING! EVERY DAY BETWEEN NOW AND NEXT SPRING, IT'S GOING TO BE RUN, RUN, RUN, RUN...

I DON'T KNOW...HE MAY BE A GOOD PLAYER, AND I'M GLAD I HAVE HIM ON MY TEAM, BUT I STILL SAY HE'S THE FUNNIEST LOOKING KID I'VE EVER SEEN!

SCHULZ

I WAS WRONG..
I CAN SEE
IT NOW...

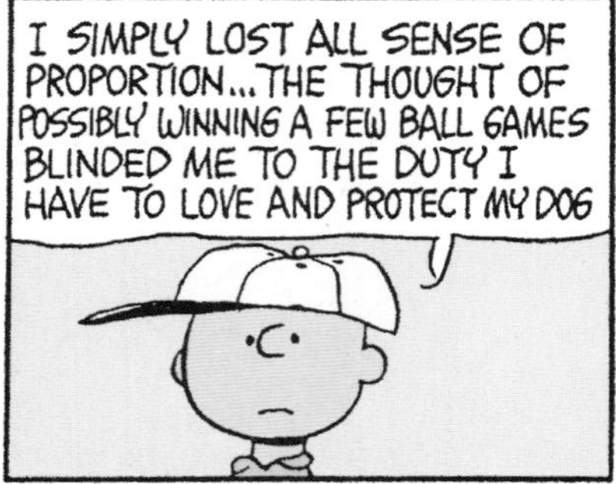
I SIMPLY LOST ALL SENSE OF PROPORTION...THE THOUGHT OF POSSIBLY WINNING A FEW BALL GAMES BLINDED ME TO THE DUTY I HAVE TO LOVE AND PROTECT MY DOG

LOOK, SNOOPY, I'M TEARING UP THE CONTRACT... I'M GOING TO TELL PEPPERMINT PATTY THE DEAL IS OFF!

WHAT DID YOU SAY?
OH, GOOD GRIEF!!
SCHULZ

!
WHAT'S THIS? YOU'VE TORN UP OUR CONTRACT, CHUCK..

YOU MUST HAVE GOT MY MESSAGE
MESSAGE?

THOSE FIVE PLAYERS I WAS SUPPOSED TO TRADE TO YOU SAID THEY'D GIVE UP BASEBALL BEFORE THEY'D PLAY ON YOUR TEAM!

SORRY, CHUCK..THE DEAL'S OFF... I HOPE YOUR FEELINGS AREN'T HURT..
I'M CRUSHED!
SCHULZ

I'VE TAKEN ENOUGH OF YOUR INSULTS, YOU STUPID DOG!

I'M GONNA POUND YOU! I'M GONNA FIX YOU GOOD!

DON'T LOOK AROUND...THERE'S NO WAY OUT! NO WAY!

YOU'VE HAD IT, DOG! PREPARE TO MEET YOUR DOOM!

SMAK!

AUGH!

WUMP!

ONE KISS IS WORTH TWO JUDO CHOPS ANY TIME!
SCHULZ

HERE'S THE WORLD WAR I FLYING ACE ZOOMING THROUGH THE AIR IN HIS SOPWITH CAMEL

I FEEL SORRY FOR THOSE POOR BLIGHTERS IN THE TRENCHES DOWN BELOW...

I THINK I'LL WAVE TO THEM...

BLIGHTERS ALWAYS FEEL BETTER WHEN YOU WAVE TO THEM!
SCHULZ

HERE YOU ARE, SNOOPY...HAPPY THANKSGIVING!

THANK YOU

NO CRANBERRIES?
SCHULZ

SNOW?!
BUT I'M NOT READY FOR WINTER!

MY BLOOD'S TOO THIN! I STILL HAVE MY SUMMER FUR!

STOP SNOWING! STOP IT, I SAY! STOP THIS STUPID SNOWING!

RATS!
SCHULZ

HOW IN THE WORLD DO YOU FIND A SNOW-COVERED SUPPER DISH?!
SCHULZ

GOOD GRIEF! IT SNOWED LAST NIGHT!

SO HERE I AM COVERED BY A SOFT BLANKET OF SNOW... I THINK I'LL LEAP UP AND SCATTER IT IN ALL DIRECTIONS...

BUT WHAT IF IT **ISN'T** A SOFT BLANKET OF SNOW?

WHAT IF I'M COVERED BY A SHEET OF **ICE**? WHAT IF I'M TRAPPED SO I CAN'T MOVE?

I'VE GOT TO LEAP UP! I'LL COUNT TO THREE AND THEN I'LL LEAP UP... ONE, TWO.. WHAT IF IT **IS** ICE? I'LL BE DOOMED! THEY WON'T FIND ME 'TIL NEXT SPRING!

BUT THAT'S NONSENSE! IT MUST BE A SOFT BLANKET OF SNOW! I CAN JUST LEAP UP, AND SCATTER IT IN ALL DIRECTIONS! BUT WHAT IF IT **IS** ICE?!

I'LL BET IT'S ICE! I'LL BET I'M TRAPPED! I'LL BET I'M ALREADY FROZEN TO DEATH! I'LL BET I'M..

HEY, STUPID, WAKE UP! YOU'RE COVERED WITH SNOW!

I'LL NEVER LEARN TO MAKE MY OWN DECISIONS
SCHULZ

REAL FIGURE SKATERS SMILE A LOT...

MAYBE JUST A PLEASANT GRIN WOULD BE BETTER..
SCHULZ

BEING A GOOD FIGURE SKATER IS HARD WORK

RIGHT NOW I'M PRACTICING MY "OUTSIDE FORWARD ROLL"

LATELY I'VE HAD TO DO MY PRACTICING AT NIGHT...

OTHERWISE I'M SURROUNDED BY FLOCKS OF ADMIRING GIRLS...
SCHULZ

ACTUALLY, THEY ALL LOOK ALIKE TO ME!
SCHULZ

"THE ORIGIN OF THE BEAGLE IS NOT KNOWN"

"THE NAME, HOWEVER, IS TAKEN FROM THE FRENCH WORD 'BEGLE'"

IS THAT RIGHT?

OUI!
SCHULZ

Z

!

THERE'S THAT DOG HOWLING AGAIN... HE GIVES ME THE CREEPS... HE HOWLS EVERY NIGHT...POOR GUY..

HE HOWLS BECAUSE SOME STUPID HUMAN KEEPS HIM TIED UP ALL THE TIME!

WHAT'S THE SENSE IN HAVING A DOG IF YOU KEEP HIM TIED UP ALL THE TIME?

LISTEN TO HIM HOWL.. GOOD GRIEF, WHAT A NOISE...WHY DON'T THEY LET HIM LOOSE? BOY, HUMANS ARE STUPID!

THERE'S NO ONE WHO CAUSES MORE TROUBLE IN THIS WORLD THAN HUMANS.. THEY DRIVE ME CRAZY... I GET SO MAD WHEN I THINK ABOUT HUMANS, THAT I COULD SCREAM!

GOOD MORNING, SNOOPY!
BLEAH!

WHAT DID I DO?
SCHULZ

HERE'S THE WORLD WAR I FLYING ACE ZOOMING THROUGH THE AIR IN HIS SOPWITH CAMEL

IT'S OUTRAGEOUS HAVING TO FLY A MISSION ON NEW YEAR'S DAY!

WHAT DO THOSE PEOPLE AT HEADQUARTERS THINK WE ARE?

ACTUALLY, I'VE BEEN UP ALL NIGHT DRINKING ROOT BEER!
SCHULZ

KER-CHUNK!

THANK YOU VERY MUCH, SNOOPY..

I WAS ALL OUT OF STAMPS
YOU'RE WELCOME

I'M THE ONLY ONE IN THE NEIGHBORHOOD WITH A POSTAGE METER
SCHULZ

IF YOU SIT THERE MUCH LONGER, THE SNOW IS GOING TO COVER YOU UP!

CRAZY DOG!

I'M NOT CRAZY..

I'M JUST WITHDRAWING FROM THE WORLD!
SCHULZ

HERE'S THE WORLD WAR I FLYING ACE ZOOMING THROUGH THE AIR IN HIS SOPWITH CAMEL..

♫ OVER THERE! OVER THERE! ♫

♪ PACK UP YOUR TROUBLES IN YOUR OLD KIT BAG.... ♫

HOW IN THE WORLD AM I GOING TO GET MY TROUBLES IN A "KIT BAG"?
SCHULZ

CHARLIE BROWN, IF A STAR FELL DOWN HERE, WOULD YOU BE ALLOWED TO PUT IT IN A PAIL, AND TAKE IT HOME?

WELL, IN THE FIRST PLACE LINUS, A STAR IS PRETTY BIG.. YOU'D NEVER BE ABLE TO GET ONE IN A PAIL...
YOU WOULDN'T?

NOPE! I'M AFRAID NOT..

SCHULZ

Z

MMMM....THERE'S NOTHING COZIER THAN A SLEEPING BAG...

THERE'S ONLY ONE THING THAT BOTHERS ME...

WHERE DO I KEEP IT DURING THE DAY?
SCHULZ

HERE'S THE "CREATURE FROM THE SEA" RISING UP TO TERRORIZE THE WORLD...

I LOVE SCIENCE-FICTION
SCHULZ

THIS KID AT SCHOOL INSULTED ME, SEE?

NOW, WHAT I WANT YOU TO DO IS BITE HIM ON THE LEG TO HELP ME GET EVEN WITH HIM..

BITE SOMEONE...JUST TO GET EVEN?

HOW GAUCHE!
SCHULZ

I WOULD HAVE MADE A GOOD SCHOOL PRINCIPAL!
SCHULZ

HERE'S THE WORLD WAR I FLYING ACE ZOOMING THROUGH THE AIR IN HIS SOPWITH CAMEL!

IT IS RUMORED THAT THE RED BARON IS IN THE AREA..

MY MISSION IS TO SEARCH HIM OUT, AND BRING HIM DOWN...

HMM.. INCLEMENT WEATHER..

GENERAL PERSHING WOULD NOT BE PLEASED IF I CAUGHT COLD!

BAM!
BAM!
BAM!

WHAT IN THE WORLD...

HERE'S THE WORLD WAR I FLYING ACE BACK AT THE OFFICERS' CLUB THROWING DARTS
SIGH!
SCHULZ

YOU SPEND ALL YOUR TIME LYING ON TOP OF THAT DOG HOUSE..

THAT'S ALL YOU SEEM TO DO... YOU JUST LIE THERE AND LIE THERE

I JUST DON'T SEE HOW YOU DO IT!

LET'S NOT OVERLOOK THE POSSIBILITY OF GENIUS!
SCHULZ

YOU KNOW, THERE ARE TIMES WHEN YOU REALLY BUG ME!

BUT I MUST ADMIT THERE ARE ALSO TIMES WHEN I FEEL LIKE GIVING YOU A HUG...

THAT'S THE WAY I AM... BUGABLE AND HUGABLE!
SCHULZ

THIS IS THE SAME THING I HAD TO EAT YESTERDAY..

IN FACT, THIS IS THE SAME THING I HAD TO EAT EVERY DAY FOR THE PAST MONTH!

I THINK I'LL REGISTER A COMPLAINT...

AFTER I'VE FINISHED EATING!
SCHULZ

WAITING FOR VALENTINES!
SCHULZ

!

THAT'S HIS "HA-HA, YOU HAVE TO SHOVEL IT, AND I DON'T" DANCE !
SCHULZ

WAITING FOR VALENTINES...

OH.....WELL, GOOD LUCK..
THANK YOU

YOU'LL NEED IT!

YOU DIDN'T HAVE TO SAY THAT!!
SCHULZ

SIGH
SCHULZ

AND I GOT A VALENTINE FROM JOYCE AND I GOT ONE FROM PEGGY

AND I GOT ONE FROM ZELMA, AND JANELL, AND BOOTS, AND PAT, AND SYDNEY, AND WINNIE, AND JEAN, AND ROSEMARY, AND COURTNEY, AND FERN, AND MEREDITH ...

AND AMY, AND JILL, AND BETTY, AND MARGE, AND KAY, AND FRIEDA, AND ANNABELLE, AND SUE, AND EVA, AND JUDY, AND RUTH ...

AND BARBARA, AND OL' HELEN, AND ANN, AND JANE, AND DOROTHY, AND MARGARET, AND...
I CAN'T STAND IT... I JUST CAN'T STAND IT...
SCHULZ

AND I GOT A VALENTINE FROM CLARA, AND I GOT ONE FROM VIRGINIA AND ONE FROM RUBY..

AND I GOT ONE FROM JOY, AND CÉCILE, AND JULIE, AND HEDY, AND JUNE, AND MARIE ...

AND KATHLEEN, AND MAGGIE, AND DIANE, AND VIVIAN, AND CHARLOTTE, AND TEKLA, AND LILLIAN, AND...
GOOD GRIEF!
SCHULZ

AND EDNA, AND NAOMI, AND LILA, AND FRAN, AND..

YOU DIDN'T GET A VALENTINE FROM LILA!
I DIDN'T? DIDN'T LILA SEND ME A VALENTINE?

LILA DOESN'T LOVE ME ANY MORE!

OH, WELL...AND CONNIE, AND CHIYO, AND MARILYN, AND AILEEN, AND..
I CAN'T STAND IT...I JUST CAN'T STAND IT....
SCHULZ

THERE'S AN ARTICLE HERE IN THE PAPER ABOUT THIS DOG...

HIS OWNER IS BEING SUED BECAUSE THE DOG DUG UP THE NEIGHBOR'S FLOWER GARDEN

BOY, YOU DOGS SURE DO SOME STRANGE THINGS

I CANNOT BE RESPONSIBLE FOR THE ACTIONS OF MY COLLEAGUES!
SCHULZ

I'M AFRAID TO GO OUTSIDE..THERE'S A VULTURE SITTING ON MY SNOWMAN!

SEE?
WELL, HE WON'T BE SITTING THERE VERY LONG THE WAY THE SUN IS SHINING...

STUPID BEAGLE!
WE VULTURES HAVE A HARD LIFE...
SCHULZ

I HATE WINDY DAYS!
SCHULZ

SOMEDAY, I'D LIKE TO PUNCH A CAT IN THE NOSE!

I WONDER IF I'D EVER HAVE THE NERVE TO TRY IT...

PROBABLY NOT

IT'S KIND OF FUN TO THINK ABOUT, THOUGH..
SCHULZ

NOW, LOOK HERE.. I DON'T THINK YOU'RE EVEN TRYING!

BLEAH!

COME BACK HERE!! YOU CAN'T QUIT THE TEAM BEFORE THE SEASON EVEN STARTS!

I SHOULDN'T HAVE ACCUSED HIM OF NOT TRYING...BEAGLE-SHORTSTOPS ARE SO SENSITIVE...
SCHULZ

WHAT'LL WE DO? SNOOPY'S QUIT THE TEAM!

ALL I DID WAS BAWL HIM OUT A LITTLE..
DON'T BLAME YOURSELF, CHARLIE BROWN...

THAT'S THE TROUBLE WITH THAT STUPID DOG...HE'S ALWAYS CHANGING RAINBOWS!

"CHANGING RAINBOWS"?!
SCHULZ

Z

CLUMP!

!

!!!!
!!!!

EVENTUALLY, I MAY HAVE TO GIVE UP KITE FLYING...
SCHULZ

PLEASE COME BACK TO THE TEAM, SNOOPY...

IF YOU COME BACK, I'LL DO ANYTHING! I'LL RAISE YOUR FOOD ALLOWANCE... YOU CAN PLAY ANY POSITION YOU WANT.. YOU CAN EVEN BE MANAGER!

MANAGER?

HERE'S THE WORLD FAMOUS BASEBALL MANAGER STANDING IN THE DUGOUT..
NOW WHAT HAVE I DONE?
SCHULZ

MANAGER?

THAT STUPID BEAGLE IS GOING TO BE OUR NEW MANAGER? NOTHING DOING! I'LL..

BOOT!

WE BASEBALL MANAGERS DON'T STAND FOR ANY BACK-TALK!
SCHULZ

STRIKE THREE!

BOOT!

THIS NEW MANAGER IS GOING TO BE ROUGH TO PLAY FOR!
SCHULZ

KLUNK!

BOOT!
BOOT!

SCHULZ

IT'S KIND OF NICE NOT BEING MANAGER..

ON THE NIGHT BEFORE OUR GAMES I ALWAYS USED TO LIE AWAKE WORRYING...

I WONDER IF OUR NEW MANAGER IS LYING AWAKE WORRYING...

Z
SCHULZ

HERE WE GO... THE FIRST PITCH OF THE SEASON!

GOOD GRIEF! A HOME RUN!!

BOOT!
SCHULZ

OH, OH! OUR NEW MANAGER IS GIVING ME THE SIGNAL TO STEAL SECOND..

"YOU'RE OUT!!"

BOOT!

WELL, WE LOST OUR FIRST GAME OF THE SEASON..

I WONDER HOW OUR NEW MANAGER WILL TAKE THIS DEFEAT ?

BOOT! BOOT! BOOT!
BOOT! BOOT! BOOT!

I HATE LOSING!

CHARLIE BROWN, WHEN A TEAM LOSES A GAME, IS IT THE FAULT OF THE PLAYERS OR THE MANAGER?

WELL, I DON'T KNOW...IT'S KIND OF HARD TO SAY, AND I...

WELL, I'M NOT AFRAID TO SAY! WHEN A TEAM LOSES A GAME, I THINK IT'S THE FAULT OF THE MANAGER!

BOOT!
SCHULZ

ACTUALLY, RUNNING A BALL CLUB IS A VERY HARD JOB

IF YOU WANT, I'LL BE GLAD TO TAKE OVER AS MANAGER AGAIN.....

SMAK!

A KISS ON THE NOSE, AND I'M OFF THE HOOK!
SCHULZ

HERE'S THE WORLD WAR I FLYING ACE SITTING ON HIS BUNK...HE IS DEPRESSED..

THIS WAR IS NEVER GOING TO END.. IT'S ALL MADNESS...IT'S INSANITY!

I NEED SOMEONE TO TALK TO..

PERHAPS ONE OF THE NURSES AT THE DISPENSARY WILL TALK WITH ME....

WELL! I WAS WONDERING HOW LONG IT WOULD BE BEFORE YOU CAME TO SEE ME...
PSYCHIATRIC HELP 5¢
AH! A DARK-HAIRED LASS... QUITE A BEAUTY, TOO! IT'S GOOD TO SEE A FEMININE FACE...
THE DOCTOR IS IN

IT'S JUST NOT NORMAL FOR A BEAGLE TO GO AROUND WEARING A FLYING HELMET..
IT'S HEART-WARMING TO THINK OF THESE AMERICAN GIRLS COMING CLEAR OVER HERE TO SERVE!
SNIF

THE FIRST THING WE HAVE TO DO IS TALK ABOUT HOW ALL THIS STARTED..
I THINK THIS LASS HAS FALLEN FOR ME ALREADY.. THE NEXT MOVE IS OBVIOUSLY MINE....... SHOULD I OR SHOULDN'T I? WHO KNOWS WHAT TOMORROW MAY BRING?

SMAK

ALL SOLDIERS SHOULD KISS AN ARMY NURSE AT LEAST ONCE IN THEIR LIVES!
SCHULZ

YOU'RE CRAZY! NOBODY CAN MAKE A SHOT LIKE THAT!

YOU THINK YOU CAN GO THROUGH THAT WICKET, AROUND THAT BUSH AND CLEAR ACROSS THE YARD AND HIT MY BALL? NOBODY CAN MAKE A SHOT LIKE THAT!

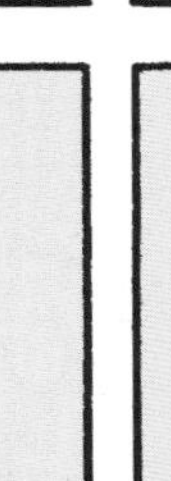
PLOK!

SCHULZ

HERE'S THE WORLD WAR I FLYING ACE OVER PONT-À-MOUSSON WITH THE EIGHTH U.S. AERO SQUADRON...

THE TIME IS 5:00 P.M. ON NOVEMBER 3, 1918... WE ARE TAKING PHOTOGRAPHS AT AN ALTITUDE OF 2200 METERS...

DOWN BELOW I CAN SEE THE POSITIONS OCCUPIED BY THE NINETY-SECOND U.S. ARMY DIVISION, AND TWO THOUSAND YARDS TO THE NORTH I CAN SEE THE GERMAN POSITIONS...

HAVE YOU EVER IN ALL YOUR LIFE SEEN SUCH GOOD RESEARCH?
SCHULZ

THERE'S A BUG IN MY SUPPER DISH...

HERE YOU ARE, SNOOPY...HERE'S YOUR SUPPER..

I WONDER IF HE TOOK THAT BUG OUT OF MY SUPPER DISH?

SURELY HE WOULDN'T JUST PLOP MY SUPPER RIGHT ON TOP OF A BUG..STILL, YOU NEVER KNOW....

BLEAH!

I DON'T WANT TO SWALLOW A STUPID BUG!

SURELY HE MUST HAVE SEEN THE BUG AND TIPPED HIM OUT... HE MUST HAVE..MUSTN'T HE?

I'M STARVING TO DEATH BECAUSE OF A STUPID BUG! MY SUPPER IS SITTING THERE, AND I'M STARVING TO DEATH, AND..

OH, INCIDENTALLY.. IF YOU'RE WORRIED ABOUT THAT BUG, I TIPPED HIM OUT

GOOD OL' CHARLIE BROWN!
SCHULZ

MORE TO EXPLORE!

Featuring cool activities and fun facts!

In addition to all these great *Peanuts* cartoons, here are some cool activities and fun facts for you related to flying, World War I and comic strips. Thanks to our friends at the Charles M. Schulz Museum and Research Center in Santa Rosa, California, for letting us share these with you!

Glossary of WW1 Flying Terms

Aerodrome: A facility that is used for aircraft flight operations, whether they include air cargo, passengers, or neither.

Blighter: A person who is pitied, in this case, someone who is fighting in the trenches.

Chocks Away: A phrase used by a pilot telling the ground crew to remove the blocks by the wheels that kept the plane from rolling away.

Dogfight: A battle between two fighter planes at close range.

Flying Ace: A military aviator credited with shooting down several enemy aircraft during aerial combat. The actual number of aerial victories required to officially qualify as an "ace" has varied, but is usually considered to be five or more.

Flying Circus: The name of the Red Baron's air unit.

Fokker Triplane: The type of aircraft used by the Red Baron's air unit.

No-Man's-Land: In World War I, each opposing side fought from a trench system. The space between the trenches, where nobody wanted to be seen for fear of being attacked, was called No-Man's-Land.

Red Baron: Manfred Albrecht Freiherr von Richthofen (5/2/1892– 4/21/1918) was a German fighter pilot with the Imperial German Army Air Service during the First World War. He is considered the top ace of the war, being officially credited with 80 air combat victories.

Sopwith Camel: The type of aircraft used by the British air units. It was highly maneuverable and very difficult to defeat in a dogfight.

Twin Vickers: The type of machine gun attached to British fighter planes.

Unter Den Linden: The iconic main street of Berlin, Germany.

Song Lyrics

Throughout this book, Snoopy often refers to song lyrics that were popular during World War I. They include:

It's a Long Way to Tipperary

Give My Regards to Broadway

Over There

Pack Up Your Troubles in an Old Kit Bag

Map of France

Snoopy also refers to many places in France throughout the book. See if you can find them on this map of France during World War I.

Paper Airplanes

Have your own aerial fun by following the instructions on this page and the next to make two paper airplanes using regular printing paper (8½ x 11).

Easy Glider

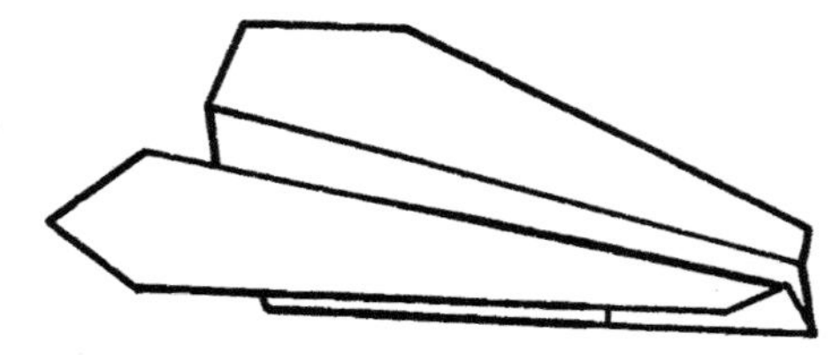

BACK

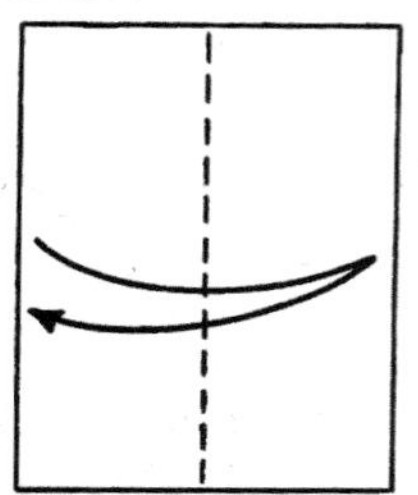

1 Fold in half side to side, then unfold.

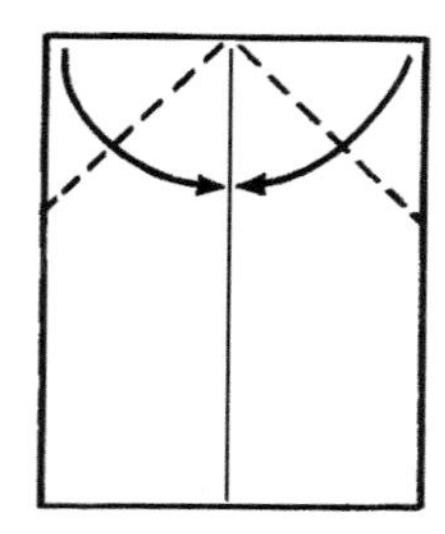

2 Fold top corners to the middle.

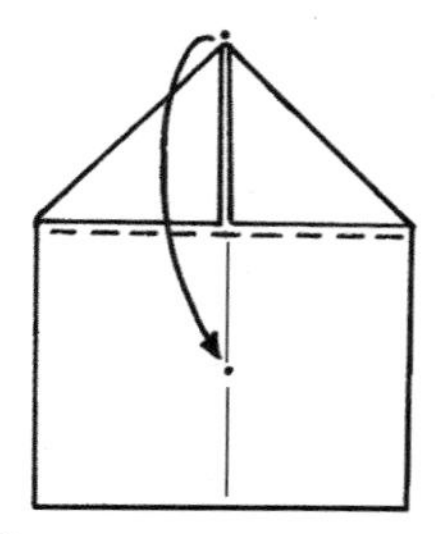

3 Fold the top down.

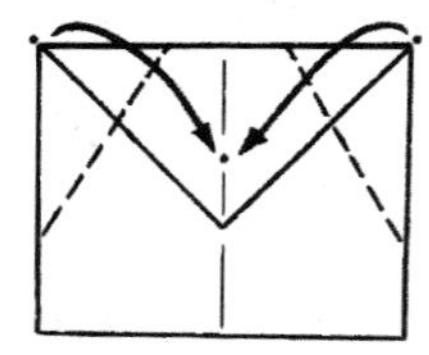

4 Fold corners down to meet at the middle.

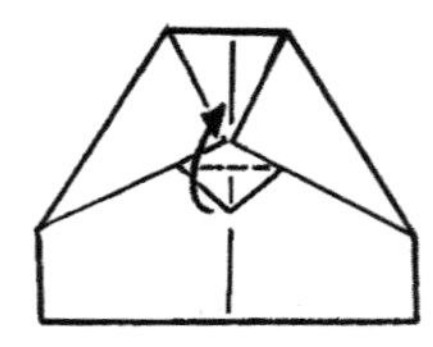

5 Fold this point up to hold the corners.

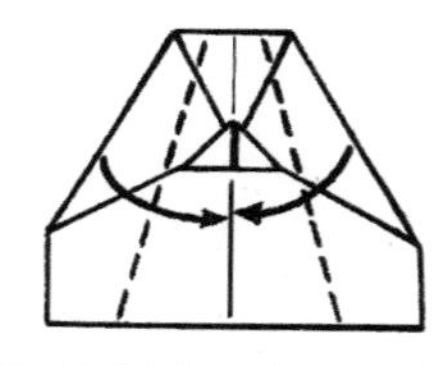

6 Fold the sides to the middle as shown.

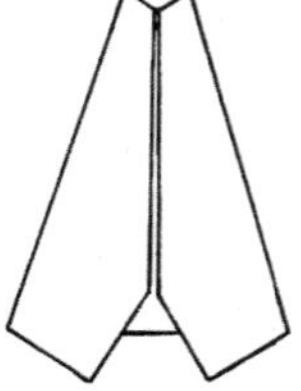

7 Your plane should look like this. Flip it over.

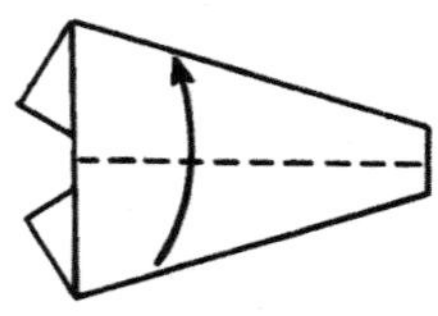

8 Turn the plane sideways and fold it in half as shown.

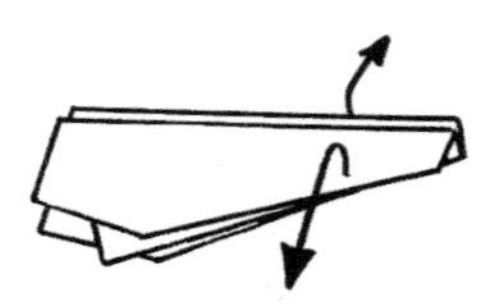

9 Open out both wings and adjust.

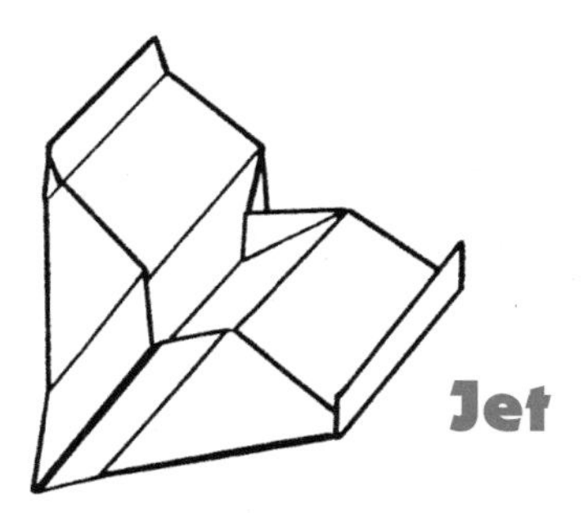

Jet

BACK

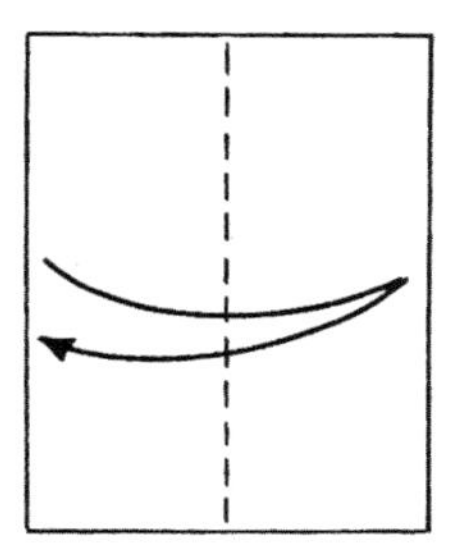

1 Fold in half side to side, then unfold.

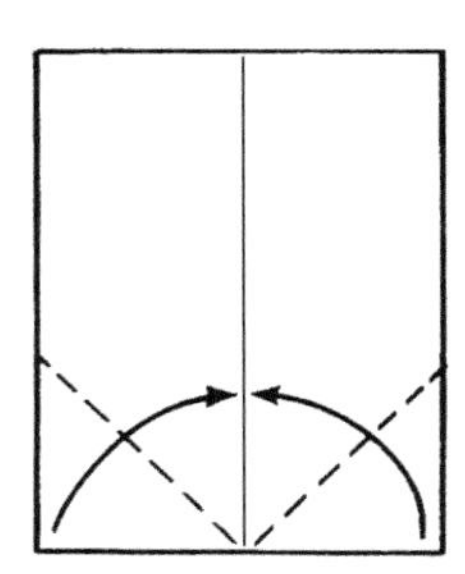

2 Fold the bottom corners to the middle.

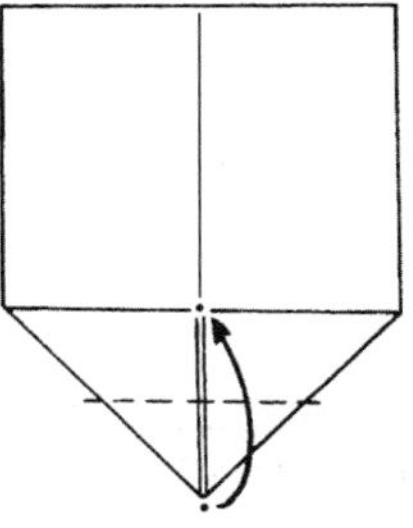

3 Fold the bottom point up to meet the edge.

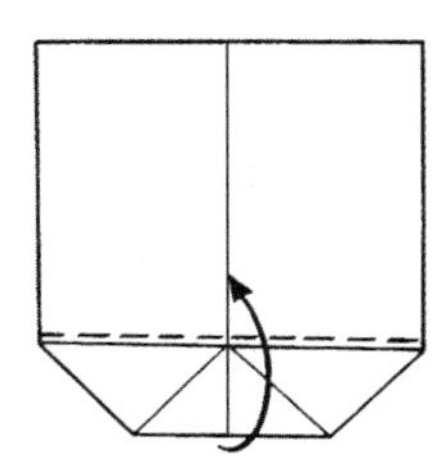

4 Fold the bottom edge up again.

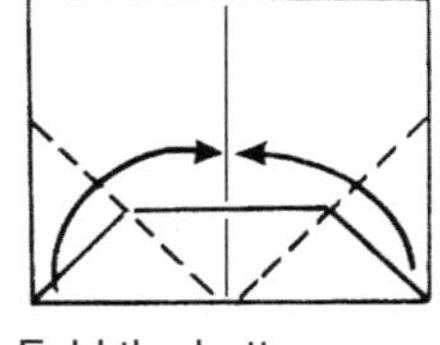

5 Fold the bottom corners to the middle.

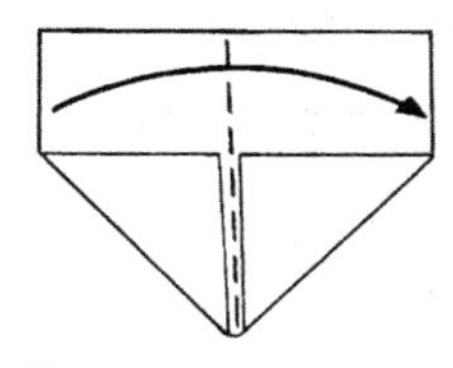

6 Fold your plane in half as shown.

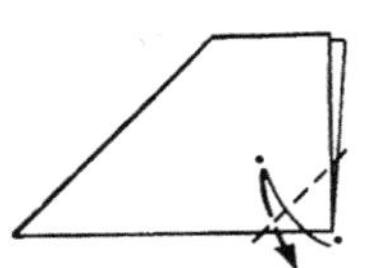

7 Turn your plane sideways. Fold back the bottom corner, then unfold.

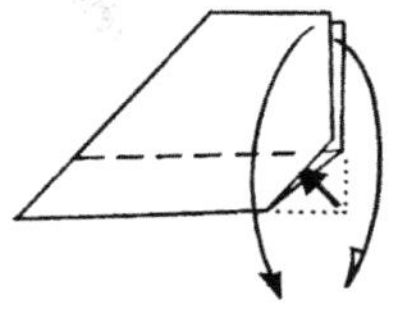

8 Push that corner in. Then, fold the wings down.

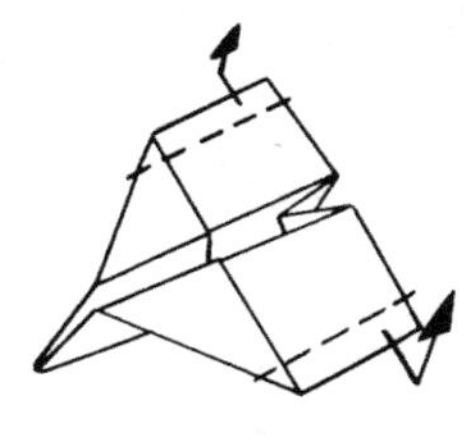

9 Fold wing tips up and adjust.

Make an Animated Flip Book

An animator must capture a broad range of movements in order for a cartoon to look continuous. Animation is possible because of a phenomenon called "persistence of vision," when a sequence of images moves past the eye fast enough, the brain fills in the missing parts so the subject appears to be moving.

MATERIALS: paper, index cards, or sticky notes; stapler and staples, paper clips, or brads; pencil or marker

INSTRUCTIONS:

1. Cut at least 20 strips of paper to be the exact same size, or use alternative materials, such as index cards or sticky notes.
2. Fasten the pages together with a staple, brad, or paperclip.
3. Pick a subject—anything from a bouncing ball to a flying doghouse or a shooting star.
4. Draw three key images first: the first on page one, the last on page twenty, and the middle on page ten, then fill in the pages between the key images.

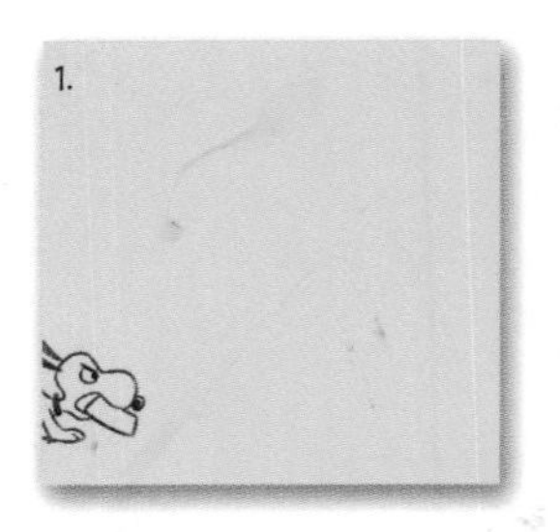

Peanuts is distributed internationally by Universal Uclick.

Andrews McMeel Publishing, LLC
an Andrews McMeel Universal company
1130 Walnut Street, Kansas City, Missouri 64106

www.andrewsmcmeel.com

www.peanuts.com

15 16 17 18 19 SDB 10 9 8 7 6 5 4 3 2 1

ISBN: 978-1-4494-7183-5

Library of Congress Control Number: 2015937248

Made by:
Shenzhen Donnelley Printing Company Ltd.
Address and location of manufacturer:
No. 47, Wuhe Nan Road, Bantian Ind. Zone,
Shenzhen China, 518129
1st Printing – 7/20/15

Check out these and other books at ampkids.com

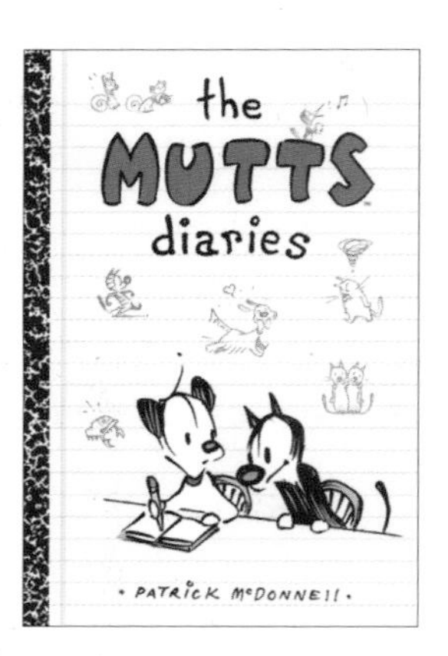

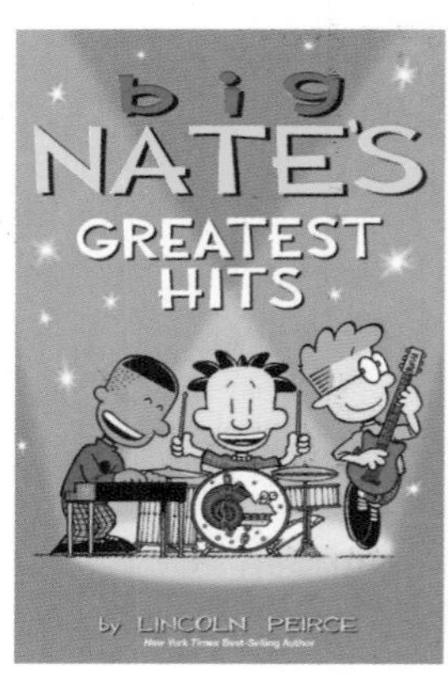

Also available:
Teaching and activity guides for each title.
AMP! Comics for Kids books make reading FUN!